DARK SPACE

(5th Edition)
by Jasper T. Scott

http://www.JasperTscott.com
@JasperTscott

Acknowledgements

Many thanks to my family, friends, and my beautiful wife, all of whom believed in me and encouraged me even when I would have rather stuck my head in the sand. You all made the journey worth the effort. And a special thanks to my team of editors! You know who you are.

To those who dare,
And to those who dream.
To everyone who's stronger than they seem.

"Believe in me / I know you've waited for so long /
Believe in me / Sometimes the weak become the strong"
—STAIND, *Believe*

Table of Contents

Prologue

A vast backdrop of stars sparkled all around Ethan's head, just on the other side of the nova interceptor's thin transpiranium cockpit canopy. The stars seemed so close he could touch them, but Ethan couldn't allow himself to be distracted by the view. He targeted the nearest enemy fighter and brought the red brackets under his crosshairs. His ears picked up the soft click of a laser lock even before his eyes registered the crosshair turning green. He pulled the trigger and held it down, pouring a continuous stream of bright red pulse lasers into his target. Then the laser charge gauges began flashing red on his HUD, and that stream of fire diminished to a slow trickle. Ethan eased up on the trigger and switched over to missiles just as his target began jinking out of line. Enemy ripper fire sizzled off his rear shields, and Ethan broke into an evasive pattern, forgetting about his target for the moment. The sound of ripper fire hitting his shields stopped, only to start again from another angle when a second junker swooped down onto his six. Ethan craned his neck to get a visual reference on the enemy fighters. They were converging on him from completely opposite directions—a pincer maneuver that was sure to get him killed.

"Ah, a little help over here? I'm caught in a vice!"

"Roger that, Five," Seven said.

Ethan tried to hold it together as enemy fire sizzled off his shields, turning them dark green, then yellow, and finally red. Now shells *plinked* off his hull as the shields were unable to completely dissipate the energy of those projectiles.

The streams of enemy fire on his port side ceased, followed by, "That got him!" from Guardian Seven. Now, with only one fighter attacking him, Ethan strengthened his shields on the starboard side and circled around to line up on the enemy fighter's tail. A few moments later he poured freshly charged pulse lasers into the twin hulls of a blocky junk fighter whose starboard maneuvering jet was already flickering dimly. Unable to evade him, the junker took heavy fire. One of his shots punched through to the reactor, and the enemy fighter suddenly exploded, sending the twin hulls flaming off in opposite directions.

"I need help!" Gina screamed.

Guardian Three came on saying, "Four enemy fighters just broke off from the main group! They're lining up for another pass on the *Defiant!* Get them before—" The comm died in static.

"Lead?" Ethan quickly checked his scopes.

A second later Ithicus came back saying, "I'm all right. Got winged by a bit of shrapnel. No major damage. Those four fired off a volley of torps at point-blank range. Dumb frekkers."

The command channel sounded in the next instant with, "Guardians, we need a better screen than that!"

"Doing the best we can, Control," Three shot back. "We're down by five and there are at least two enemy squadrons out here. Where are your gunnery crews?"

"Cannons are coming online any minute."

We don't have a minute, Ethan thought to himself. "Six,

where are you?" he asked, remembering that she'd called for help. He spent a moment checking his scopes for Gina without any luck. A cold fist seized his heart, but then he found her, cutting an evasive pattern toward the *Valiant*, a pair of enemy interceptors pouring golden streams of ripper fire on her tail. Those two were fast for junkers—she was having trouble shaking them.

"I'm right where you left me, you dumb kakard! I don't suppose I still have a wingmate out there somewhere?"

Ethan grimaced. He wasn't used to working in teams. "Sorry, on my way now." He came about and boosted with the last of his afterburners to catch up to the enemy interceptors. Once in range, he switched to hailfire missiles and quickly dropped one on the enemies' tails. A second later he realized his mistake as he noted the proximity between the enemy interceptors and Gina's own nova. "Gina, get out of there! I just fired a hailfire on your pursuit."

"Frek you! My afterburners are tapped out! What do you want me to do?"

Ethan thought fast, even as the blue trail of the hailfire's primary thrusters winked out. The enemy fighters realized their peril and broke off from Gina to go evasive, but they were still too close.

"Reverse thrust!" Ethan said.

"They might lock on to *me* if I do that!"

Frek, Ethan thought. "Hold on!" He thumbed over to pulse lasers and targeted the distant missile, hoping he could get it before it exploded into its four smaller warheads. At this range his targeting computer refused to lock onto the missile. Desperate, Ethan raked blind laser fire over the target brackets. Nothing happened. An instant later, the hailfire exploded in four separate directions, and Ethan felt a stab of fear. Sweat trickled into his left eye and he swiped at it with the back of one hand, blinking to clear his vision. The smaller warheads flared to life and boosted after the enemy fighters.

"They're too close!"

Ethan could hear a tremor in Gina's voice. "Give me a second!" he said, switching fire to the warhead arcing closest to Gina. He hit it with a lucky shot, and the resultant explosion tore into the nearest enemy fighter, drawing flames and debris from its thruster pods. Gina's fighter rocked in the shockwave. Then the other three warheads found their marks, and the remaining two enemy fighters exploded in blinding fireballs. Ethan heard Gina scream, and then her comm cut off in static. "Gina!"

The static hissed on and Ethan felt a horrible chill creeping down his spine.

Frek! His heart pounding, Ethan checked his scopes, but they'd fuzzed out due to the proximity of the explosions. He flew through the expanding fireballs and ignored the sound of debris pelting his fighter. His forward shields quickly dropped into the red, and he feared what that meant for Gina. "Gina!" he tried again.

Then he saw her, one of her three engines still glowing, the other two flickering. Her starboard stabilizer fins had been knocked off, and he could see her cockpit canopy was striated with fractures. "Gina, for Immortals' sake, answer me!"

A moment later her voice came back to him, but she sounded weak. "I'm alive. Took a hit through my canopy. My suit's pissing air."

"Krak, how badly are you injured?"

"Not much blood, but breathing hurts like a motherfrekker. Maybe a few broken ribs."

"Fly back to the *Defiant*. I'll cover you."

"I'll never make it, not on half thrust. . . . Too many enemy fighters."

Ethan gritted his teeth. "Well, frek it! You're just gonna give up and die?"

No answer.

Ethan watched the hull of the *Valiant* growing large before them. In his periphery he spotted the *Defiant's* beam cannons opening up as the cruiser made her first pass on the *Valiant's* port hangar. Eight blue dymium beams shot out, drawing rippling waves from the hangar's shields.

A few seconds later, Ethan saw nova fighters tearing out of the carrier's launch tubes.

"Are those our novas coming from the *Valiant*?" Gina asked.

Ethan shook his head. "We don't have anyone left on board. We took everyone except for the sentinels with us."

"So those are *enemy* novas. Frek!"

Ethan had no reply for that. By now Brondi had overwhelmed the six sentinels in the concourse between the carrier's ventral hangars and he was taking control of the ship—including its considerable compliment of nova fighters and interceptors. *Gina's right. We won't make it back to the Defiant.*

No one will.

A DEAL WITH THE DEVLIN

TWO DAYS EARLIER . . .

Chapter 1

Ethan Ortane stood at the smeary viewport, looking out at space through a greasy sheen of fingerprints. His fingerprints. He placed a hand against the viewport, adding a fresh smear of grease. Here and there against the blackness of space a bright blue or orange glow of real space drives flickered to life as some or other ship fired its engines to change course, speed up, or slow down. They were easy to pick out against the blackness of Dark Space—the distant sector of the galaxy where humanity had holed up since the war. Dark Space was a cluster of black holes with a small pocket of semi-habitable planets and stations inside. Radiation was a constant threat, and if you weren't in a reasonably shielded station or ship, you would be burned alive. Some of the planets were far enough away and had strong enough atmospheres that they didn't bake in the radiation, but most were inhospitable rocks. For these reasons, and because there was only one known way in or out of the sector, Dark Space had once been a place of exile for criminals, but now it was all that was left of the once galaxy-spanning Imperium of Star Systems.

Now, the ISS was dead in all but name. Only a handful of fleet vessels had survived the war, and they were left guarding the deactivated space gate which was the only way in or out of

Dark Space.

"This is what we've come to—" Ethan said, turning from the viewport with a sigh, but he wasn't talking about the galactic situation. "—renting a room in the cheapest station we can find, hiding from Brondi's collection agents until we can miraculously come up with the money to pay our debts."

Alara offered him a pretty smile from where she was sitting on the bed, and her big, bright violet eyes shone in the wan, flickering light of the room's sole glow panel. She had long dark hair and alabaster white skin with full red lips. A man could lose himself staring at her face for too long; it was like staring into a fire—you just knew that if you got too close you were going to get burned. Her face was to die for, and she had a body to match, but most of the time Ethan didn't notice either.

"Hiding is still better than dead," she said.

Ethan frowned, his eyes skipping around the dismal, boxy room. Paint was peeling off the walls; a rickety, squeaky bed lay to one side, and a low-res holo projector was mounted on the opposite wall. The room had a tiny bathroom with a vaccucleanser so small you had to step in sideways. Ethan turned back to the greasy smear of a viewport. "It's only better than dead until someone finds us."

Alara Vastra was his copilot and long-time partner in crime. She liked to play the optimist, but the truth was, without a miracle, they were both as good as dead. They'd borrowed 10,000 sols from "Big Brainy" Brondi to fix their ship after their drives had cut out and they'd crashed during a routine landing on Etaris. They'd skipped the last three loan payments in order to avoid having their ship impounded for unpaid docking fees, and now Brondi wanted them dead. They'd lost a few inches of duranium and their shields in their last encounter with his collections agents, and they didn't have the money to repair the shields. Next time they met with Brondi's agents would be the last.

Ethan spotted the characteristic ternary blue engine glow of a fighter as it jetted past the station. He idly traced its path with a pair of fingers, and then he realized what he was looking at, and his brow furrowed curiously. That was a Nova Fighter. *What are you doing out here, little guy?* Ethan wondered. Novas were the Dark Space police—aging fighters from the *Valiant*. In the last decade of hiding in Dark Space, the *Valiant's* original complement of 144 Nova Fighters and 144 Nova Interceptors had been whittled down by the slow attrition of time, firefights with the delinquent denizens of Dark Space, and by a limited supply of available replacement parts. Now there were rumored to be less than 80 of each still operational. That left a little more than one fighter and one interceptor to guard every station in Dark Space, except Supreme Overlord Dominic had permanently assigned a whole squadron of each around the fuel mines of Etaris and the farms on Forliss—not to mention the garrison at the Dark Space gate.

Translation: there were no police in Dark Space. People had to fend for themselves and settle their own squabbles. So what was a nova doing all the way out at Chorlis Orbital?

Ethan watched the fighter come around and begin an approach pattern. "He's going to dock," Ethan marveled.

Alara joined him at the viewport to see what he was talking about. She recognized the fighter immediately. "Now there's a rare sight. Must be something serious. Novas don't fly around for fun."

Ethan nodded. "I'd like to know what's up." He turned away from the viewport, heading for the door.

"Wait," Alara said. "I thought we were supposed to be

hiding."

He turned from the door to face her. "We are, but as long as we're being hunted by an infamous crime lord, I thought we might like to inform the authorities, just in case they'd care to do something about it."

Alara just stared at him with those big violet eyes of hers. "Aren't you going to ask if I want to come?"

"Do you?"

She turned her mesmerizing eyes away from him to walk over to the room's only storage cabinet. Ethan watched her open the cabinet on a squeal of rusty hinges and pull out a hefty plasma pistol. She checked the charge, and then promptly strapped it around her waist. Ethan was already wearing his. Closing and locking the cabinet, Alara turned back to him, and said, "Let's go."

Chapter 2

Ethan and Alara walked past a parade of rusty duranium doors with peeling paint and barely legible room numbers on their way through the darkened corridors of Chorlis Station. Half of the station's glow panels were dark while the other half were flickering. Even as they walked, Ethan saw sparks fly from one of them as it flared and went out. The corridors were deserted, but every now and then they could hear the despondent moaning or angry screaming of the residents beyond those doors. Ethan frowned. While most of the stations in Dark Space weren't in good repair, renting a room aboard Chorlis Station was the equivalent to crawling into an armpit— and humanity had already holed up where the galaxy's many suns didn't shine.

"What if that nova is here looking for us?" Alara whispered.

They walked past door number five and heard a plasma pistol go off. Alara turned to the door in horror, and she slowed her pace. Ethan grabbed her arm and pulled her along.

"Don't slow down," he growled.

"I think someone just killed himself!" Alara said in a disbelieving whisper.

"Or someone else."

They heard the *swish* of a door opening behind them, and turned to look just in time to see a bald, dark-skinned man emerging from door number five and holstering a steaming plasma pistol. He was dressed entirely in black. "What are you looking at?" the man said.

Ethan froze, his hand dropping automatically to his sidearm. "Nothing. I mind my own business," he said.

The dark man eyed them for a moment, taking in the fact that both of them were armed. "Smart," he said, and his hand drifted away from his gun.

Ethan nodded and dragged Alara around a bend in the corridor, his heart pounding with adrenaline. Dark Space might be lawless, but for the most part people weren't looking for trouble. At least, not trouble they couldn't handle.

"Ethan," Alara said in a frightened tone. "What are we doing? We are fugitives just as much as Brondi is. Going to the authorities won't help."

"Everyone in Dark Space is a fugitive, and besides, I'm not trying to sick the novas on him. I'm more interested in finding out if the *Valiant* has any work for us."

"Why would you . . ." Alara trailed off with a sly smile. "Oh you're a devlin, Ethan. If I'd known you were so smart, I would have agreed to marry you when you proposed to me."

Ethan frowned. "I was drunk, and you said you were leaving. It's not easy to find a good copilot."

"Oh, come on, why don't you just admit it. You know you love me," she said, leaning on his arm and resting her head on his shoulder.

He turned to look down at her, and then he waved his hand in her face to indicate the silver band on his ring finger. "I'm already married, remember?"

Alara let go of him and looked away with a fading grin. "Right, I almost forgot."

"Anyway," he sighed, changing the topic. "My idea is, if we're employed by the *Valiant*, it's going to be hard for Brondi to get to us. We might even get an escort out of this nova pilot."

"It's a brilliant plan," Alara said absently as the corridor they were walking down opened up into a combined lobby and bar for Chorlis Orbital's one and only functioning habitat module.

Ethan turned to look at her, but she'd turned away to look out the wall of viewports which made up the far side of the lobby. Out those viewports Ethan could see the station's hydroponic module; the green fronds of plants pressed up against the dirty transpiranium dome. It looked inviting, but they didn't have time to stroll through the gardens and catch a breath of fresh air.

Alara wandered over to the viewports, while Ethan walked up to the bar. He planned to stay here and wait for the nova pilot to come to him. Everyone who came to Chorlis Orbital eventually ended up at the bar, and usually sooner than later. There wasn't much else to do.

"Drink?" the bartender asked as Ethan pulled out a bar stool and sat down. The barman had a lumpy face and a glowing red tattoo whorled around one eye. He looked like he'd seen a lot of brawls in his day. Maybe he was an ex-con from Etaris, same as Ethan.

Ethan reached across the counter and bared his wrist. The bartender scanned his embedded identichip with a wand, and Ethan said, "Just a water, please."

"Sure," the bartender said with a smirk. He busied himself by typing something into the wand, and a moment later, a total flashed up before Ethan's eyes.

Water - 3.00 sols, Chorlis Orbital.

The transaction was relayed from the chip in his wrist directly to his brain and then flashed up like an afterimage before his eyes. Ethan cast a quick look over his shoulder to see if Alara was coming to join him at the bar, but she was standing statuesque by the viewports.

Ethan frowned. He could hardly blame her for being upset. They were friends—friends and partners in business, but nothing more, and she obviously wanted more. It wasn't as though she hadn't tried or he hadn't been tempted, but as he'd said, he was married. Eleven years ago he'd been exiled to Dark Space for smuggling, leaving his wife and young son behind.

The following year the ISS had mapped a hyper route through the Devlin's Hand, the giant red nebula which lay in the gulf between their galaxy and the neighboring satellite, The Getties Cluster. The ISS was foolish enough to link the two galaxies with space gates straight away, and before they were even done exploring the solar system on the other side, they were under attack. The massacre which followed quickly spread through the gate, from one galaxy to the other, and took trillions of lives.

To this day, no one knew why the war had started or even much about the insectile aliens who'd started it. One theory was that the Sythians—or "Skull Faces"—had run out of habitable space in their small satellite galaxy, and they'd just been waiting to find a way to cross the void between galaxies. Once a pathway had been opened up, the war had ended in just nine months. The Sythians hadn't had a technological edge, but they'd had greater numbers, better coordination, and they'd used cloaking shields to hide their ships until the last minute before attacking, always taking Imperial forces by surprise.

And while the Sythians' SLS (superluminal space) drives weren't as fast as the Imperium's SLS drives, their cloaking devices had enabled them to use the ISS's network of space gates without anyone being the wiser.

In the time it took for a baby to be born, humanity had been all but annihilated. A lucky few had managed to evacuate to Dark Space, but the coordinates of the gate were uncharted. Worse, it was hidden in a statically charged ice cloud that disrupted sensors, making it impossible to find the gate unless you already knew where to look. Apparently those who had known about the gate hadn't shared that secret with the downtrodden masses, so the majority of the evacuees who had arrived were high-ranking fleet officers and government officials.

But that hadn't stopped Ethan from searching among the survivors. As soon as the gate leading out of Dark Space had been deactivated and sealed, and after all the "non-dangerous" prisoners had officially been released to help support a flagging economy, Ethan had wasted two years of his life searching for a familiar face—on the off chance that either his darling Destra or little seven-year-old Atton had been able to escape the war, but he hadn't been able to find either of them, and eventually he'd been forced to give up the search for a lack of funds. What had followed was a dark period for Ethan, but four years ago Alara had come into his life, and with her quick wit, easy smile, and those beautiful violet eyes, she'd managed to mostly snap him out of it. But that didn't mean he was ready to move on—or that he'd like to move on with her. She was young enough to be his daughter!

There was no doubt that in some way he needed Alara. Without her he was lost and everything ceased to have its meaning. He needed someone to be counting on him—someone to need him and value him, and even to love him. He just wasn't sure he could ever love her—not romantically anyway. She was young. She'd find someone else. Until then, they'd have each other to rely on and to keep one another company.

The bartender slid a spill-proof, shatter-proof mug filled with Ethan's water across the counter. He nodded his thanks, to which the bartender grumbled something unintelligible. A hand landed on his shoulder, interrupting him as he took a sip of his water. He turned to see Alara standing behind him. "I'm sorry," she said.

Ethan shook his head and frowned. "For what?"

She sat down on the bar stool beside him and reached for his water. "About your wife and son," she said as she took a sip from his mug.

"Don't worry about it," he said gruffly. "That was a long time ago."

"I'm not finished yet," she said in a warning tone. "I *am* sorry, but you can't live the rest of your life in mourning for them. You've got to be happy, Ethan. They would have wanted that for you."

Ethan smirked. "You're asking me to be happy with a garbage scow of a light transport, more debt than the damn thing is worth, and a rat hole that we can barely afford to pay for." He shook his head. "May as well ask me to grow wings and fly."

"No," she said sharply. "I'm asking you to be happy with *me*." She reached out to stroke his stubbly cheek, her eyes searching his. "We're in this together, Ethan. The least we can do is act like it." She traced a line down his cheek, following a scar he'd acquired in an old prison fight. Her exotic violet eyes were full of emotion, but his were dead and unseeing.

Ethan looked away. He felt a familiar numbness spreading through him at the mention of his wife and son. A moment later, Alara seemed to realize she was talking to a wall. Her hand fell from his cheek and she turned away, too. "I guess we can go on the way we are. No strings attached. Just business, right?" She flashed him a heartbroken smile.

He tried to smile back, but the sentiment never reached his eyes. "I think that's best, Alara. I don't want anybody else to get hurt."

She nodded. "That's okay. It was a stupid idea. Don't pay attention to me, Ethan."

He nodded absently, his eyes still unseeing. He ended up staring into a bottle of ice blue Shirali Wine while sipping his water, untold minutes passing until his peripheral vision caught a flicker of movement off to his right. Ethan turned and saw a brawny nova pilot strut in with his helmet tucked under his arm. The pilot couldn't have been more than 18 years old; he stood too straight, and he reeked with the arrogance of youth. The nova pilot jerked his chin at the barman. "I'm looking for a man dressed in black."

The barkeeper snorted and gestured to his own mostly black attire. "You gonna be searching a long time with that description."

"Black skin, too. Goes by several aliases. You might know him as Verlin. He's a contract killer, a bounty hunter. He killed an Imperial officer a few weeks ago."

The bartender shook his head. "Sorry. Can't say I've seen anyone like that."

Ethan's eyes narrowed thoughtfully. "Hoi!" He raised a hand and waved to the officer.

The young man frowned and crossed the room. He

stopped a few feet away, and his eyes flicked meaningfully up and down Ethan's patched and faded flight suit. "Yes, grub?"

Ethan felt his temper rising, but with an extraordinary effort he managed to clamp down on it. "What's the information worth to you?" Ethan asked.

The pilot frowned, and his bristly blonde hairline arched down with his eyebrows. "It's worth *not* arresting you for trying to bribe an officer with information that could lead to the capture of a dangerous criminal."

Ethan shrugged and turned back to the bar. "Oh, okay. Just wondering."

The nova pilot stared at him a moment longer before offering a reply. "I could have you locked up."

Ethan turned back with a smile and held out his wrists. "Great, where do I sign up?" It was an old trick, and the fleet was long since tired of it. There were enough career criminals floating around Dark Space that it was impossible to lock them all up, and a fair number of them actually wouldn't mind being locked up in exchange for three square meals and a place to lay their heads. For just about anyone, that would be a vacation. This nova pilot was obviously too young to have seen much of that yet, so he just stared at Ethan with bemusement.

That was when Alara chimed in, saying, "You've gone and got his hopes up. Now you're going to have to follow through."

The nova pilot shook his head. "You grubs are crazy. Do you have information for me or not?"

Ethan withdrew his wrists with a crooked grin. "Tell you what, you give me some information and I'll give you some."

"You can ask, but that doesn't mean I'll answer."

"Fair enough. Is the *Valiant* hiring? I have a light freighter with an empty hold, just waiting for a job."

The nova pilot shook his head. "I wouldn't know, but the overlord likes to manage his own supply chain within the fleet. More reliable. No offense, but we don't need the likes of whatever beaten up scow you're flying to transport goods that are worth more than the hold they'd be flying in."

"And what about pilots? I'm rated 5A, and my copilot here," Ethan said, jerking a thumb over his shoulder to Alara, "can handle just about any secondary and tertiary ship functions that you can think of."

The nova pilot shook his head again. "I'm sorry, but we have more applicants than ships, and I don't believe you have a 5A rating. These days you can fake your rating for the price of a good meal—not that I think you have the money for either."

"I can prove it."

"Sure you can. Stop wasting my time. If you want to enlist, go visit a recruitment office. You have information about my man or not?"

Ethan drained his water and rose from the bar counter with a tight smile. "Not."

The young nova pilot gritted his teeth and reached for his sidearm. Ethan's hand was already on the butt of his. "I wouldn't do that if I were you," Ethan said, nodding to the nova pilot's pistol. "How do you think I got to be this old?" He pointed with his right hand to his vaguely graying hair. "I bet you a month's pay I'm a faster draw than you are."

"Are you threatening me, grub?"

"I wish you'd stop calling me that. Makes killing you sound better and better all the time, and I really don't need the extra incentive."

Ethan felt Alara's hand on his shoulder and heard her whisper his name in a warning tone. The bartender watched the developing confrontation with a shadowy grin.

The nova pilot held Ethan's gaze a moment longer before letting out a snort of laughter. "Nice try, but you're going to have to shoot yourself if you're that tired of living. Move along. You're not my objective."

Ethan noted with a smile that this time the young pilot didn't refer to him as a grub—a nickname for low-class citizens whose only concern is their namesake—grub, food, *survival*.

"Thought you might say that." Ethan began backing away and offered a mocking salute with his right hand, while his left stayed near his plasma pistol. "You're too young and pretty to die."

"Ethan!" Alara whispered sharply beside his ear, but he was past caring.

Desperation and despair do wonders for a man's courage, he thought. *You're not afraid to die if life's not worth living.* That was one of the reasons why the fleet tried to stay out of civilian affairs. They had a cushy lot by comparison, and they had much more to lose.

The nova pilot looked on with a scowl, but he said nothing.

Once Ethan had backed up to the bend in the corridor which led back the way they'd come, he turned around and began walking swiftly to their room.

"So much for that!" Alara said. "If I'd known you were planning to play chicken with an Imperial officer I wouldn't have bothered coming with you."

Ethan shrugged. "I wasn't planning on it, Alara, but krak happens sometimes, you know that."

She snorted. "More often around you."

"Hoi, have some respect, kiddie."

Alara turned to glare at him. Ethan pretended not to notice. "Besides, we did get something out of that nova pilot."

"Oh? And what's that?" Alara asked.

He turned to meet her gaze. "A way out. We're going to enlist in the fleet."

Chapter 3

"Join the fleet?" Alara demanded. "Are you completely skriffy?" She was lying on the bed in their room again; her jaw hung open in exaggerated shock, and her arms were crossed over her chest. "What about the *Atton*? We're just going to throw it away after we put so much work into it? We wouldn't be in debt right now if it weren't for your damn ship! We wouldn't be hiding here. I could've had a life on Forliss, instead of this." She gestured to the peeling walls around her.

Ethan was standing by the viewport, his eyes and thoughts wandering out into space. He didn't have the energy required to face Alara's angry tirade, so he stayed silent, his thoughts processing his plan without her until she came down from her wailing, emotional high and talked to him in a more rational tone.

"This is unbelievable! If you could've just had this idea a few months ago, we wouldn't be in this mess. I could've gone back to work in the agri-domes with my parents, and you could have thrown your life away all by yourself—instead of dragging me down with you. I don't know why I stay with you! I must be sick. That's it. I must have some sick screw loose that makes me gravitate toward a grub like you."

Now Ethan did turn from the viewport, and his eyes glittered darkly at her. "I'm sorry, what was that?"

"Nothing," she mumbled, shaking her head. "I didn't mean it." Alara looked up at him miserably. "I'm just angry—at our situation, Ethan. Not at you. I'm sorry. I take it back."

He walked up to the foot of the bed. "No, it's too late for that, Alara. Sorry isn't wide enough or deep enough to cover up the truth. So that's what you really think of me. You think I'm a grub."

Ethan held up a hand to stop her next objection, and he pressed the other one to his forehead to massage away an encroaching headache. His eyes squinted shut and he took a long moment to answer her.

Alara stood up from the bed and walked over to him. She laid a hand on his shoulder and stood up on tiptoes to kiss his cheek. "Please forgive me."

He turned, opened his eyes, and shook his head. "Why *are* you with me, Alara?"

"Ethan . . ."

He took a step back and she took one forward, but he gently pushed her away. "No, you know what, you're right. You don't need a grub like me holding you back. You were born for more than this." He gestured to the boxy room with a sneer. "Your parents are big shots in the agri corps; you could go back to them just like you said. You were one of the lucky ones until you struck out on your own—now you're just an upper-class snob trying to live the common life. It's a joke, Alara, and no one's laughing at it. You'll be better off with them."

Alara gaped at him.

"Besides, if you want to make your own way, you can do better. Pretty girl like you could make a good living in a pleasure palace," he said, and she flinched as if he'd slapped her. "Or you could go pro and find some rich husband in Brondi's gang. Wouldn't that be ironic."

Alara shook her head. "You don't mean that."

"Sure I do. You said it yourself, you don't need a grub like me holding you back. You need to move on to bigger and better things. I understand. Go to sleep, Alara. I'll wake you in the morning. I wasn't planning to sell the *Atton*, but since I've been such a dead weight for you, seems like that's the only fair thing to do. I'll drop you on Forliss Station, sell the ship, pay off your half of the debt we owe Brondi, and you'll be free to go live your life."

Alara looked more hurt than ever, and now Ethan could see tears shimmering in her eyes. "Frek, Ethan, I didn't mean it! You're hurting me!"

He smiled thinly and brushed by her on his way to the door. "I'll be at the bar if you need me."

He opened the door with a wave of his hand, and she whispered after him, "I've always needed you, Ethan. It's *you* who doesn't need *me*."

* * *

Ethan Ortane was a man of his word. Despite Alara's protestations, the next morning he charted a course straight from Chorlis Station to the Forliss System. The final space gate in the series plotted by the nav dropped them right on top of Forliss Station. From there, if she wanted to, Alara could book passage to the surface of Forliss and join her parents working in the giant agri-domes, or else she could stay on the station. There were plenty of hydroponic modules for her to work in agriculture if she wanted to, but there was also plenty of just about everything else. The station stretched out for kilometers in every direction, lighting up space with a million twinkling lights. Cylindrical mall and market modules joined with spindly arms to spherical hydroponic modules, which in turn joined to circular hubs that were connected to blocky habitats, hangars, and office spaces. Forliss Station was one giant city in space, hastily constructed, and poorly thought out, but big enough for a person to get lost—both literally and metaphorically.

Ethan lined his ship up with the blinking green docking buoys, and stopped at the inspection point. While he waited, Ethan transmitted his ship's remote access codes to the station, and then a nova fighter popped by and ran a quick scan on them. Once they were cleared by the Nova, the docking controllers acknowledged receipt of his codes and gave clearance for Ethan to enter the station's landing pattern.

As soon as the station's pilots took remote control of his transport, Ethan turned to Alara and said, "Well, I guess this is goodbye."

Alara sat back in her chair and crossed her arms over her chest. "I guess so." Her voice sounded so flat and despondent that Ethan felt the need to comfort her.

"Look, all hard feelings aside, this is what's best for both of us. You're right. You don't deserve to be saddled with my debt. It's my ship after all."

She turned to him then. "We racked up that debt together, Ethan."

"Well, consider it a gift, then. I'm joining the fleet, and Brondi can't easily touch me there. This way, at least one of us is still free."

Alara nodded silently and turned back to look out at the stars. Ethan wasn't sure what else he could say—what she *wanted* him to say—so he looked away, too. The station grew larger and larger before them until they spotted the amber glow of the hangar deck where they were being directed. Ethan watched the transport ahead of them duck inside the station, and then the station's pilots took them in next, using the hangar's grav guns to guide them straight into the nearest empty berth.

The station's docking tube snaked out toward them. It connected resoundingly with their hull, and a cheery message came over the comm, "Welcome to Forliss Station! We hope you have a pleasant stay."

Ethan slung his travel bag over his shoulder, shut down his ship's reactors, and walked aft. Alara was just a step behind him. He reached the amidships airlock and keyed the control panel to cycle it open. The inner airlock door opened with a hiss of equalizing air pressure, and Ethan walked inside.

"So that's it?" Alara demanded from the other side of the airlock. "After three years of friendship, you just drop me off at the nearest station, sell your precious ship, and enlist in the fleet?"

Ethan offered her a helpless shrug. "What you want me to do? We don't have a lot of options. You could always join me in the fleet."

"You might get in because you're a *rare* '5A' pilot," she made quote signs in the air with her hands. "But I don't have any special skills, Ethan. What I do as your copilot, a trained monkey could do."

"You don't give yourself enough credit, but there's no other option, Alara. I'm sorry."

Alara shook her head. "No, you're wrong, there *is* another option."

Before Ethan realized what she meant, she'd slapped the

control panel, and the inner airlock door was cycling shut.

Ethan lunged for the narrowing gap, but airlock doors were made to open and shut quickly, and he wasn't about to risk having an arm chopped off for his trouble. So instead, he devoted himself to the control panel on the inside of the airlock, but as soon as he tried to key it open with his password, it spat out an error message and beeped angrily at him. With a dawning horror he realized his mistake. He'd thought Alara's silence along the way had been out of sadness, but hers had been a vindictive silence, and somehow, when he hadn't been looking, Alara had changed the ship's entry codes. He tried waving his wrist over the identichip scanner, but the control panel sounded with another error beep.

Ethan looked up to see Alara smiling and waving at him through the small square of transpiranium set in the top of the airlock door. He pounded on it with his fists. "Let me out!"

She cocked her head and regarded him dubiously. "Are you sure?" she mouthed. The airlock was soundproof.

Ethan gritted his teeth and hit the door one more time for emphasis. The dull thud of his fist echoed through the ship, and abruptly Alara seemed to make up her mind. She tapped another sequence into the airlock controls, and the outer door cycled open. Alara gestured to it meaningfully, and he scowled back at her.

She was stealing his ship. He couldn't believe it! It wouldn't get her anywhere, though. Even selling it, he wouldn't have been able to pay off the entire debt to Brondi, and he'd been willing to use the entire sum of money to pay off Alara's half of the debt, so this really wasn't any different to him, except that now he didn't need to find a buyer and haggle for a decent price. He'd miss some of his personal belongings, but he didn't have a lot of those. As a prisoner on Etaris, he'd gotten used to keeping all the important stuff with him in the old brown travel bag which was already slung over his shoulder.

Ethan cast a quick look to the open airlock behind him and the waiting docking tube, then he turned back to Alara, pursed his lips, and nodded. *If that's the way she wants it, fine.* He gave her a curt salute, and then turned and walked away.

Chapter 4

Ethan didn't look back. Alara hadn't expected him to, but if he had, he would have seen the tears running down her cheeks, and then maybe he would have understood that she wasn't being hateful or spiteful; she was trying to save him from himself. He'd catch up with her later, after he realized what a mistake he was making, and then she'd return his ship to him, and they'd go on as they always had—

Together.

When Ethan disappeared from sight, Alara turned and walked back through the ship. Rather than go to the cockpit and fly off immediately, she went to the lounge and lay down on the sofa bed to quiet her racing thoughts.

What have I done? was the first thought which ran around in circles in her brain. *He'll be back,* was the second. And with that thought, she managed to calm herself enough to fall into a troubled sleep.

* * *

Once Ethan started down a road, he never looked back. It was looking forward he sometimes had trouble with—whether that meant moving on from his wife, Destra, or simply looking to the future with something more than abject pessimism. He hadn't always been like that, but being sent to the mines of Etaris, ripped away from his wife and son, and being forced to face facts with a life sentence for smuggling stims, Ethan hadn't become a big believer in hope. Then the war had come and ripped the galaxy to pieces, so pessimism seemed like a good bet.

The fact that he still maintained some small bit of hope that he might someday run into his wife and son again was the one glimmer of optimism that proved the pessimistic rule of his life. Nobody had to sugarcoat things for him. He was used to staring cold facts in the face, and the cold fact was, his partner and only friend in the universe had just betrayed him and stolen his ship. Prior to that she'd called him a *grub* and said she was better off without him.

I guess loyalty only runs so deep, he thought as he made his way around one of the many circular hubs aboard Forliss Station. *By now, she's probably halfway back to Chorlis Orbital so she can go back to hiding from Brondi.* He wasn't sure what she planned to do with his ship now that she had it all to herself, but he wasn't sure he cared either. Out of respect for the partnership they'd once had, he hoped for her sake that she didn't run into any collection agents on her way back. She wasn't a half bad pilot, but not nearly good enough to shake off pursuing fighters with no shields and no copilot to man the guns. She'd be captured for sure, and knowing Brondi, he wouldn't let her die easy.

Well, that's her problem. Ethan switched his focus to the task at hand. He knew that there was a fleet recruitment office somewhere aboard Forliss Station. The trick would be finding it. The station was a maze of twisting corridors, and they shot off at all angles from the circular hub where he was now walking. Each corridor had an illuminated sign above it which described the module waiting immediately on the other side, but that didn't tell Ethan what modules were waiting on the other side of those, and further still down the line. Ethan sighed and stopped walking in order to get his bearings. The nearest corridor branching off the hub went to *Yuri's Café*, the next one around the bend, to the *Summer Gardens*.

Ethan turned to the nearest passerby and raised his hand to get the man's attention. The man wore a shiny black suit—business attire—and he was walking fast. When he saw Ethan walking toward him, he sped up, but Ethan kept pace with him easily.

"Do you know which way to the fleet's recruitment offices?"

The man shook his head quickly. "No, sorry."

Ethan frowned. "Do you know where I can find the nearest station directory to look them up?"

"No."

"Hoi, you must know where I can find a directory at least. You live here, right?"

The man turned and gave him a disparaging sneer. "Get away from me, grub."

Ethan grabbed the man's arm and spun him into the nearest wall, pinning him there. "What did you call me?"

"N-nothing."

"Where is the nearest directory, you little kakard?"

The man pointed to a corridor that branched off the hub up ahead, the one whose sign read, *Summer Gardens*. "Through there! Now let me go! *Please.*"

"All right, no need to piss your pants. I'm leaving." Ethan gave the man a shove, causing him to stumble and almost fall, and then Ethan turned to walk toward the gardens, but he still kept half an eye on the man he'd accosted. The businessman didn't seem like the type to be armed and dangerous, but sometimes weakness was a guise, especially if it were worn too conspicuously. Looking defenseless and being defenseless were two very different things in Dark Space, and mistaking the one for the other could make you dead.

As the businessman hurried around the corner, Ethan finally turned his back and strode into the Summer Gardens. The corridor branching off the hub was long and narrow. There was a moving walkway going in each direction, and up ahead a strange brightness illuminated the walkway.

The corridor soon arced out over the gardens and opened up, becoming a bridge. All around him the fresh, moist air swirled with the fragrances from a dozen different flowers in full bloom. Birds flitted over the bridge, twittering and chirping. Below and all around, the green fronds of leafy trees reached high into the artificial sky, which was a clear, cheerful blue overhead. Ethan sighed. If the pay were a little better, it would be worth being a parks and recreation officer just to have such a relaxing work environment. It sure beat having to breathe the canned, almost bitter air pumped out by shipboard recyclers.

The bridge wound slowly down into the gardens below, and soon Ethan was walking through the gardens at ground-level. He could reach out and touch the leafy greenery rising all around him. He stopped to admire a gigantic blue crystal flower. The petals were thick, and from what he knew, they were actually edible. Taking a quick look around to see that nobody was watching, Ethan snapped off a petal and popped it into his mouth. The flower fruit exploded in a burst of citric-sweet flavor that was a painful reminder of why freeze-dried rations were only for the poor grubs who couldn't afford fresh. Nobody would willingly choose such bland garbage over this. Ethan snapped off another petal, and this time a tired mechanical voice berated him. "Please pay for your purchase." The voice was loud, and Ethan looked around again to make sure he hadn't drawn attention to himself. No one was watching, so he hurried off.

Ethan shook his head. *I knew it was too good to be free.* He eyed the scanner bar which ran all around the cultivated gardens. It was cleverly disguised as a railing, but now that he looked at it closely, it contained the telltale red glow of a sol scanner. If he passed his wrist over it, he had no doubt it would deduct the required amount from his account.

Ethan wound his way around the cultivated jungle, looking for an exit. Supposedly, somewhere in here there was a station directory, but he hadn't seen one so far. The businessman had probably just lied to get rid of him.

Come on, Ethan thought as he rounded another bend in the winding garden paths. The path he was on opened into a square with a cascading fountain in the center. The fountain was overgrown with climbing blue-flowering plants that seemed to flourish in their aquatic home. They'd wormed their roots into the synthstone, cracking it and crumbling pieces off the statue which sat atop the fountain.

Ethan stopped to survey his surroundings. Branching off the square were four different pathways which wound through the dark, shadowy greenery of the gardens. *Someone could get lost in here for hours,* he thought. Perhaps that was why nobody else was walking through the gardens with him. The place was huge. Ethan turned in a slow circle, his eyes skipping around, searching for someone, anyone—an agri-worker or another pedestrian just passing through like him, but everywhere he looked there were just plants and empty synthstone paths. Suddenly he felt the hair on the back of his neck prickling, and he heard a voice call out behind him—

"Looking for someone?"

Ethan whirled around with his hand already on his gun to find himself face to face with the dark man he'd seen aboard Chorlis Orbital. "Hands up, Ethan." The dark man nodded to Ethan's sidearm. "Drop that at your feet and kick it toward me. Slowly."

"How do you know my name?" Ethan asked nonchalantly as he slowly drew his weapon and dropped it as instructed. He purposefully ignored the last part of the dark man's command and didn't kick the weapon away from himself.

The dark man shook his head. "Not relevant."

Ethan tried another tack. "What are you doing here?"

A new voice joined them then. "The better question, Ethan, would be what are you doing to get me my money?"

Ethan whirled again, unable to believe his ears. Standing behind him with a wide, toothy grin on his pudgy face was none other than Big Brainy Brondi himself. The crime boss had an annoying habit of smiling with his mouth open, like he was always on the brink of bursting into laughter. "Do you have it?"

Ethan shook his head slowly. "No, but, hoi, Brondi, I can get it for you. I was just about to sell my ship to get you the money. Swear to the Immortals that's what I'm here for."

"Not nice to lie, Ethan," Brondi said, smoothing a hand over his head of slicked back black hair. "My man, Verlin, had a talk with a very agreeable nova pilot who was more than happy to spill his guts." Brondi gave another gaping smile and stared at Ethan with over-wide, bloodshot gray eyes that suggested heavy stim use. "Literally and figuratively, that is.

Seems like you were planning to run away and join the fleet, isn't that right, Verlin?"

Ethan smiled in an attempt to lighten the mood. "Look, just give me a couple more hours. I'll sell my ship, and you'll have your money. You can come with me, if you like."

Brondi raised his eyebrows in an exaggerated fashion, and his gaping smile broadened until it looked like he was trying to swallow a giant burger whole. "Yes! Yes, that's right. I'll come with you. Then you can sell your ship for half the money you owe me, and I'll kill you to make myself feel better about the other half. But wait!" He frowned and began tapping his chin. "What was the name of that ship you acquired this morning, Verlin?"

"The *Atton*."

An icy dread slithered into Ethan's gut.

"Isn't that your ship, Ethan? The one you were planning to sell?"

"Where is she, Brondi?"

"Where is who?" The crime boss asked with an unconvincing look of innocence etched across his fat face. "Oh, you mean your copilot! Verlin—" Ethan watched as Brondi seemed to be trying to peer over his head to get Verlin's attention. It would have been comical were the situation not so serious, since Brondi was only about five feet tall.

"Yes?" Verlin answered, and Ethan turned to half look at the bounty hunter.

"I can't recall. . . . Did you have to kill the woman on board that ship, or did she surrender the vessel willingly?"

"She fought back, but she's alive."

Brondi placed a hand on his chest and staggered back, as if a great weight had suddenly been lifted from his boxy shoulders. "Thank the Immortals! What a relief! For a minute I thought . . . well, never mind what I thought—the important thing is that she's alive!"

"Release her to me, Brondi, and I'll get you your money."

Brondi's eyebrows arched sharply downward. "No, no, no, that's not how this works, Ethan. And besides, how do you propose to get me my money if you no longer have a ship to sell?"

Ethan gritted his teeth. "You can't steal my ship and still pretend I owe you 10,000 sols. The ship is worth at least six."

"Who said anything about stealing? I said we *acquired* a ship, Verlin. Does that sound like stealing to you?"

Verlin didn't answer, but Ethan noted a return of Brondi's gaping smile. "It's all about the way you package things, Ethan. Why be so negative?"

"It's my ship, you dumb frek!"

Brondi's smile faded instantly and suddenly his bloodshot eyes were cold and stony. "No, Ethan. It's my ship. Consider it the interest on your backdated loan payments. I should have you vivisected for speaking to me that way, but I'll let it go."

Ethan's eyes were locked on Brondi's, meanwhile he pictured the garden square in his head, looking for an escape route. Behind him, one of the paths was cut off by Verlin. In front, Brondi had closed off the way he'd come. To either side were another two paths, apparently open, but Ethan knew better than to trust that. Brondi wouldn't be here without his usual cadre of bodyguards. That was why the gardens were deserted. Brondi had all the entrances and exits sealed up, just as he surely had people waiting down all the ways out of the square. Not to mention that making a run for it would open him up to fire from Verlin, and the man had to be a crack shot to make a living as a bounty hunter in Dark Space. Escape wasn't an option.

"Did you come all this way just to kill me, Brondi?"

The crime boss spread his hands. "No, I came all this way to acquire a new vessel for my fleet, and to find a man who owes me a great debt, so I can offer him a deal."

Ethan's eyes narrowed. "What kind of deal?"

"I'll scratch your debt, and release your pretty little copilot, and I'll even let you chase your dream of becoming a fleet officer. Sound good so far?" Brondi's eyes were glittering madly in the artificial sunlight.

"What's the catch?"

"Catch? What catch? I just need a small favor. Two small favors, perhaps."

"Spill it, Brondi."

"Don't be so hasty. I'll explain, all in good time, my friend, all in good time, but first let's go enjoy a nice cool beverage aboard my corvette so we can discuss business with a little more privacy."

Chapter 5

Brondi led the way through the *Kavarath*, an old ISSF seraphim-class corvette, while Verlin and his cadre of bodyguards kept a tight watch over Ethan. Even though Ethan's hands were bound with stun cord, Brondi wasn't taking any chances.

They came to the living room aboard the corvette, and Verlin pushed Ethan down into an armchair while Brondi went to the bar counter in one corner of the room to fix their drinks. The room was a big open space with clean, opulent white furniture. Ethan spent his time studying the lavish appointments of the corvette and idly adding up the probable prices of the furnishings in his head until he reached some absurd number and stopped, disgusted by the gross excess. Brondi's corvette was richly adorned with deep blue carpets, soft, recessed gold glow panels, elaborate moldings on the white walls and ceiling, priceless fireglass sculptures—their crystalline depths roiling with rainbow-colored light—and even more priceless paintings from a bygone era when people still had the money for art. It was a painful reminder to Ethan of how the other half lived. Well, the other one or two percent, anyway.

"You know, Ethan, if you had agreed to work for me all those years ago, you could have shared in this," Brondi said, gesturing to the walls around them. "I could use a pilot as good as you."

"I was a smuggler once, Brondi. I lost everything because of that. I won't make the same mistake twice."

"Yes, yes, we've all heard the sad stories. You got caught, went to prison, leaving your wife and son behind. Blah, blah, blah! Wake up, Ethan! You have nothing to lose any more! And Dark Space is no place for an upstanding citizen. You can eat caviar with the sinners, or starve to death with the saints."

Ethan watched Brondi crossing the room with two steaming glasses of a luminous red cocktail. If Ethan had to guess, he'd say it was spiked with some or other stim. He resolved not to have more than a few sips. Brondi passed one of the glasses to a blocky bodyguard, who in turn handed it to Ethan.

"Because I'm such a fair man, I'm going to give you another chance, Ethan. Fly for me, and I'll solve all of your problems. What do you say?"

"Do I have a choice?"

Brondi offered another gaping grin. "Not if you like to live."

"That's what I thought."

"Good, well now that that nasty bit of motivation is out in the open—" Brondi raised his glass, and waited for Ethan to do the same. "—to a hopefully long and mutually profitable partnership." Ethan frowned and they drank together, but Ethan didn't take more than a tiny sip of the fragrant, red cocktail. It was thick and syrupy sweet, steaming with fragrant vapor from dry ice, and glowing with some kind of phosphorescent powder that was suspended inside. Even with that small sip, Ethan felt his mind clear and his thoughts sharpen. He also relaxed considerably. The drink was definitely laced with stim, though without knowing exactly what kind of stim, Ethan was wary of the effects. He set his glass down on the transpiranium table between himself and Brondi. "I want to see Alara before we negotiate anything."

Brondi nodded agreeably, and then clapped his hands and lifted his head to speak to the ceiling. "Holofield on, level one." The air around them shimmered, and suddenly Ethan was somewhere else; he was still seated, but everywhere he looked the walls had turned from white to an ugly gray, the soft gold of recessed lighting had been traded for a dark and dreary blue light coming from an unshielded glow strip running around the ceiling. There was a strange, keening sound coming from somewhere nearby, while before him lay an empty bunk with dirty white sheets, a small viewport showing the black of space, and an open toilet in the corner. The scene was intimately familiar to him—he was locked inside a cell. A sudden feeling of claustrophobia swept through him, and he spun around, looking for an exit. That was when he saw that the keening sound was coming from a small, crumpled form lying curled up on the cold floor in front of the bars of the cell. Dark hair was splayed out around the woman's head, and her cheeks were wet with tears. Ethan felt a blinding rage welling up inside of him. He walked carefully over to Alara and bent down to touch her shoulder, but she couldn't feel his touch. What he was seeing was real enough, but his presence was an illusion. He turned to get a better look at her face, and that was when he saw the ugly purple bruise which had caused one of her eyes to swell shut.

Abruptly the holofield cut out and Ethan was staring into Brondi's loathsome features once more. Ethan's eyes went wide and bulged with fury. He tried to lunge across the table, but strong hands pulled him back and held him in place. Brondi began smiling again, and he clucked his tongue like a chicken. "Don't make me lock you up, too, Ethan."

"You hurt her!"

"No, Verlin hurt her, and she was the one who decided to resist. Be thankful that he didn't hurt her more permanently. Now, listen carefully, because I'm only going to say this once, and I'm growing impatient. I have in my possession a nova pilot's uniform, his security credentials, his identichip, a holoskin, and a vocal synthesizer implant. I also have his nova fighter."

Ethan shook his head, uncomprehending. "And you want me to . . . what? Impersonate a fleet officer?"

Brondi clapped his hands quietly. "Kavaar! You're not as dumb as you look. Yes, that's exactly right. Verlin here went to a lot of trouble to get the novas on his tail so we could acquire all of these items."

"What for?"

"Come, come, Ethan. I thought you were smart. Surely you can imagine the value of my infiltrating the fleet. Imagine the things I could do if I had someone on the inside working for me. Why, I could probably assassinate the Supreme Overlord! That would give me a great deal of personal satisfaction, although I suspect he would be replaced by someone just as annoying. Another possibility would be for me to gather Intel on any fleet operations that might compromise my activities. . . . but you know what I really want? I want the fleet gone. Poof." Brondi mimicked an explosion with his hands. "What do you suppose the Imperial fleet would be without their precious *Valiant?* There would be no one left to stand up to me. The last, feckless remnant of the ISS would be extinguished, and Dark Space would finally and truly be free of its meddling influence."

"We'd descend into anarchy," Ethan said.

"What makes you think we aren't already living in anarchy? The only difference would be no more taxation, and no more bloated fleet to drain our precious resources. Have you ever stopped to think that they don't contribute anything? The fleet doesn't produce anything, their officers eat our food, burn our fuel, and use our women, but they never give anything back."

"They give us security by guarding the gate, and they protect us from ourselves by defending the mines, farms, and factories. Without that little bit of discipline, we'd tear ourselves apart."

"They don't need to guard the gate; in case you hadn't noticed, the gate is broken down and disabled; no one bothers to maintain it anymore, and that's to say nothing of the gate on the other side. As for the mines, farms, and factories you speak of, those are already owned by rich companies. They can pay for their own defenses with the taxes they'll save. No, I'll be doing all of us a favor. Did you know that there are over 50,000 crew lounging around aboard the *Valiant?* They never do anything. The *Valiant* never moves. They just sit there, having a big party on their five kilometer-long cruise ship, all the while they reassure us that they're using up our resources to guard a gate which doesn't even need guarding, and meanwhile we are starving to death for the privilege of being able to sleep soundly at night, for the empty reassurance that they give us, reminding us of what we already know: *Don't worry, the back door is securely shut! We checked for you. Sweet dreams.* It's been shut for a decade! And if some drooling Sythian ever figured out how to open it from the other side, the *Valiant* wouldn't even see them coming."

Ethan frowned. He had to admit, as much as he might hate Brondi, the man had a point. They might actually be better off without the fleet to suck them dry. He still didn't like it, but it wasn't as though he had a choice.

Ethan pursed his lips, hesitating just long enough to assure himself that he had no other options. "So what's your plan?"

"Good!" Brondi rubbed his hands together and grinned. "See, this is why I wanted you to work for me. I don't have to explain things twice with you. The plan is simple. You infiltrate the overlord's precious carrier and sabotage it."

"You want me to kill 50,000 people."

"Don't think of it as killing 50,000 people, think of it as killing 50,000 leeches on society, and saving the hungry mouths that they are taking food from everyday."

Ethan grimaced. "After that, you'll release Alara and clear my debt?"

Brondi nodded. "I'll even give you your ship back."

Ethan hesitated. He was signing a deal with the devlin himself. In exchange for his soul, and a weight his conscience could never bear, he'd rescue Alara and himself, too. Were their two lives worth more than 50,000? But Brondi was right about one thing—50,000 fewer mouths to feed would result in 50,000 fewer people starving from the perpetual scarcity of food.

"One last question."

Brondi's forehead wrinkled up to his slicked back black hair. "Yes?"

"Why me?"

"You owe me, you're resourceful, and you're the only pilot

good enough to impersonate a nova jock without additional training."

"Hmmm. Before I go, I'd like a chance to say goodbye to Alara. Just in case. And your assurances that you'll let her go if I die in the attempt."

Brondi's eyes became cautious. "Now, Ethan, you know I'll only release her if you succeed."

"I may succeed, but not survive."

"Oh, well in that case of course I'll honor my end of the bargain."

Ethan frowned and pursed his lips, wondering if the crime boss would actually honor the deal under any circumstances, but he wasn't in a position to make further negotiations, and he didn't have a choice. "Fine, it's a deal, Brondi."

Brondi's wild eyes lit up, and he raised his glass once more. "Excellent! Drink up, Ethan. Don't waste it. That brandy costs more than 100 sols per glass."

Ethan reluctantly raised the noxious concoction to his lips once more, eyeing it all the way there. How much damage could a few doses of stim do to him anyway?

"To a brighter, freer future for Dark Space," Brondi intoned.

Ethan nodded. "To the future." And with that, they drained their glasses together.

Chapter 6

Ethan walked down the narrow corridor of the detention level aboard Alec Brondi's corvette. The detention deck was the lowermost of the ship's four levels, and it struck a noticeable contrast with the rest of the corvette's lavish appointments. Here, every expense had been spared; the glow panels were flickering, the walls were peeling, and bare conduits and pipes were visible both beneath the floor grating and running along the ceiling. The detention level was noisy and hot from the ship's reactors on level two. Ethan shuddered to think of Alara spending any amount of time down here.

They reached her cell after just a few moments, and Ethan found her just as he had seen her in the holo recording, curled up in a fetal position on the floor in front of the cell door, her hair splayed out around her head, and her face purpling with a nasty bruise around one eye. Again, Ethan felt rage welling up inside of him, but he had to force it down. While he was surrounded by Brondi's bodyguards, there was nothing he could do to avenge himself on Verlin.

Ethan went down on his haunches in front of the cell,

getting to eye level with Alara. Her eyes were shut, and her previously loud sobbing had quieted to a soft sniffling.

"Alara," he said in a gentle tone. "It's me, Ethan."

She looked up at him with grease-smeared, tear-stained cheeks. Only one of her violet eyes opened, but her gaze quickly found him and settled on his face. "Efan . . . they got you, too. I'm sawy." Her lip was split and swollen, causing her to lisp. Ethan vowed to tear Verlin apart for what he did to her. Had he known when he'd first run into the bounty hunter aboard Chorlis Orbital that the man would do this to Alara and ultimately deliver them both to Brondi, he would have drawn his sidearm and shot the dark man dead rather than saying, *"I mind my own business."*

"Hey, beautiful. How are you doing?" Ethan asked.

"How do I wook?" Alara asked. She propped herself up on one elbow and tried to smile, but it came out looking sad and crooked.

Ethan smiled back for her sake, but all he really wanted to do was cry and scream and kill. Most of all he wanted to kill. He felt like someone had just beaten his daughter to a pulp, and now he was just a few feet away from the man, and he couldn't do a thing about it. "You don't *wook* too bad," he said, trying to make fun of her lisp to lighten the mood.

"You should see the other guy," she replied, still trying that crooked smile.

"You mean me?" Verlin asked, and Alara's gaze wandered behind Ethan to the group of men standing there.

"Speak of the devwin," Alara said, and her gaze slid back to Ethan's face.

By a great force of will Ethan managed to keep from turning around and lunging at the bounty hunter. He went on smiling, but his eyes had grown cold with murder. "Look,

Alara, I'm going to get you out of here. I've cut a deal with Brondi. He's going to let us go, erase our debt, give us our ship back . . . Everything is going to be just fine. You and me again, kiddie. Like always."

"Wike always . . ." Alara repeated dreamily. Then abruptly she snapped out of it. "Efan, what are you talking about?"

"I cut a deal. We're going to get out of this, you'll see."

"What kind of deal?" Alara asked, already suspicious.

Ethan hesitated. "Don't worry about it." He rose to his feet, and Alara's good eye followed him, big and scared and suspicious.

"Efan . . ."

"It's all been taken care of."

"Listen to the man, Sweet Thing," Brondi interrupted. "He's prepared to do a lot for you."

Alara began shaking her head. She rose shakily to her feet and reached through the bars of her cell to grab hold of Ethan's hand. She managed to press on the bandage on his wrist and he winced. Realizing that something was wrong, she turned his hand over and saw the bandage. "What did you woo to him?" she asked, her gaze turning accusingly on Brondi.

The crime boss shook his head. "It's a long story."

"They removed my identichip, Alara. I'm going to impersonate a fleet officer in order to . . ." Ethan trailed off there, unable to completely say what his mission would be for fear of what Alara would think of him. "In order to get some information for Big Brainy here."

Alara shook her head. "Don't woo it."

Ethan grimaced, and pulled his hand free of hers. "I'll be back soon, kiddie." With that, he turned and began to leave.

"I love you!" she called after him.

Ethan stopped and slowly turned; his gaze met hers, and

he watched the tears shimmering in her good eye, making it shine bright like lavender blossoms in the sun. He held her gaze for a long moment before quietly saying, "I love you, too, Alara." He took a step forward, but Ethan felt hands on his shoulders turning him roughly away.

"Touching," Brondi said, "But I'm afraid it's time for Ethan to go. Say b-bye, Sweet Thing."

Ethan growled as they dragged him away. "Let me go, Brondi!"

"Oh, come," Brondi said. "I've been more than patient and understanding with you, but your mission can't wait any longer. You'll have plenty of time to frek your girlfriend when you get back."

Ethan shot Brondi a deadly look. "It's not like that."

Brondi raised his eyebrows and shook his head. "Well, I don't really care what it's like, now do I? Move along. You have a lot of prep work left to do."

UNDERCOVER

Chapter 7

Ethan watched the translucent blue swirl of the Forliss-Etaris space gate rapidly growing larger in the distance. He could hear his nova's engines roaring, and feel them thrumming through the light duranium and berlium alloy frame of the needle-nosed fighter. The joystick vibrated in his hand as he rocketed toward the Forliss-Etaris gate. Piloting a nova was vastly different from piloting a transport. There was a constant feeling of too much power for too small a ship, of acceleration that bled through the inertial management system—light G-forces the nova purposefully didn't block in order to help orient a pilot in space. There was also the fact that he had enough firepower under his trigger finger to blow up a small station. It was a wonder that the fleet didn't abuse that power more—few had the strength to stand up to them.

Ethan double-checked his nav. The star map appeared as an overlay on his HUD, and he saw the route the computer had plotted for him—from Forliss to the Etaris System, from Etaris back to the Chorlis System, then on through the Firebelt Nebula to the Chorlis-Firean gate, and from there to Firea, the ice ball where the *Valiant* lay in high orbit to guard the entrance of Dark Space.

Estimated travel time was just over an hour. The space

gates were mostly all close together, so he didn't have to spend a lot of time in real space unless he wanted to go sightseeing.

An hour wasn't much time, but hopefully it would be enough for him to review his identity and familiarize himself with the nova's controls. Ethan sat back in his flight chair and ran a hand through his recently cropped salt and pepper hair. A holoskin could fake your appearance by projecting a holo field around you, but it couldn't fake tactile sensations, and if anybody had happened to run a hand through his previously long hair, they'd have figured him out pretty fast. He wasn't planning to mingle or get close enough for anyone to pick holes in the finer details of his cover, but they couldn't rule out the possibility.

Ethan's new name was Lieutenant Adan "Skidmark" Reese, Guardian Five. He was 21 years old, characterized as arrogant, rude, and reckless. His parents worked in the agri-domes on the surface of Forliss, and he had no close relationships among the crew of the *Valiant*, except for his wingman, Lieutenant Tedris "Blaze" Ashtov, Guardian Six.

The last woman he'd dated was a member of his squadron. She was Marksman Gina Giord, Guardian Four. His squadron commander was Lieutenant Commander Vance "Scorcher" Rangel. Most of Guardian Squadron was out on patrols across Dark Space, but just in case, everything about everyone was detailed in an electronic dossier which Ethan had loaded into the holocard reader implanted behind his ear. That file had been hastily put together from interrogating the real Adan Reese who Ethan had run into aboard Chorlis Orbital. It had taken just one night for Verlin to find out everything they needed to know about the officer's life in order to steal it from him. Ethan mused that the young man must've been easy to crack, either that, or Verlin's interrogation methods were particularly effective.

Ethan closed the file with a thought and rather focused on the stars, watching them sparkle and burn. He wasn't the type to read manuals and instruction booklets. He preferred just to dive in and figure things out. He figured the best thing for his cover would be to keep his mouth shut and listen. If you gave people enough chances, they would happily tell you everything you needed to know about them. His role would be to quietly observe and stick to himself as much as possible until he could find an opportunity to sabotage the *Valiant*—that wasn't going to be easy, and escaping afterward would be even harder.

Ethan frowned. He wasn't sure he would be doing humanity a favor. In a time when the human population was already struggling, he was going to kill off 50,000 men and women. Surely there was a better way.

Maybe he could force them to become productive members of society. If he could simply doom their ship to a slow death in some way that would give them enough time to evacuate, but not enough time to fix it, then they could always find other jobs and eventually become less of a drain on society—win-win. He didn't see how Brondi could object. The mission was to take out the *Valiant*, which he *would* do. Killing the crew was implied, but not necessarily a required part of that objective.

Now the Forliss-Etaris gate was all Ethan could see in any direction, and he was racing toward the translucent blue portal at a frightening speed. "Good luck," he wished himself. "You're going to need it." And then time dilated with an actinic flash and a ripple of shimmering light.

* * *

As Ethan flew through the last and most dangerous part of the Firebelt Nebula, his eyes skipped between the nova's gravidar and his HUD, which was supposed to bracket any asteroids as soon as they appeared in range. The nebula had claimed more than a few unwary ships in the past decade because its roiling red clouds swirled with fast-moving asteroids which were often the size of planetoids. Due to the nebula, it would take him almost half an hour in real space to cross from the Etaris-Chorlis gate to the Chorlis-Firean gate— that gate was actually still inside the nebula, but it provided a safe route thanks to the string of interrupter buoys which had been seeded along its jump path. The buoys would drop Ethan out of SLS at the first sign of an asteroid coming too close. At that point, he'd have to use his own SLS drive to reinitiate the jump, which would be more fuel expensive than using a gate, but still infinitely better than being dead. In real space, the nebula's asteroids were far enough apart that they were a rare sight, and that lulled most pilots into a false sense of security while they were flying, but Ethan wasn't about to let that happen to him. He was flying his nova hands-on and eyes open.

It wasn't long before he was rewarded for his vigilance and half a dozen yellow bracket pairs of unknown gravidar contacts appeared against the distant red clouds of the nebula. An instant later, however, those contacts were identified as ships rather than asteroids. Ethan frowned at the SID codes which appeared beneath the bracket pairs. Abruptly, two of the yellow bracket pairs turned to green, indicating that they were friendly ships, and then the nebula flashed with yellow ripper fire and the other four bracket pairs turned red. The friendly targets were identified as nova fighters, while the enemy targets were listed as an "unknown type."

The comm crackled with static, and then roared with chatter.

"He's getting a missile lock on me!" The pilot's voice was female, and Ethan's targeting computer automatically identified the speaker as Guardian Four—Gina.

"Try to shake him. I'm going to drop a hailfire on his tail." That one was identified as Guardian Three, one of the many pilots whose names Ethan hadn't bothered to memorize from his file.

Great, Ethan thought dryly. He'd already run into a pair of pilots from his squadron, and one of them was none other than his cover identity's ex-girlfriend. Ethan keyed his comm cautiously, hoping the vocal synthesizer Brondi had found for him would do its job. "This is Guardian Five, you two need a hand?"

"Frek . . ." Guardian Four muttered. "I thought you were out on assignment, Five?"

"I'm back now."

"Well get over here," Guardian Three put in. "We stumbled on a pirate base out here, and they've got teeth." As if to emphasize that point, a stream of ripper fire roared over the comm, and Three began swearing viciously.

"Acknowledged," Ethan said, and fired up his nova's dymium lasers. He barely had an hour in the cockpit of a nova and he was already flying into combat. *Looks like I'm going to have to prove my 5A rating after all.* Ethan lined up the first enemy under his targeting reticle and watched as the reticle flickered green and emitted a soft tone. He pulled the trigger and three fire-linked red lasers flashed out toward his target with a high-pitched squeal that actually made his fighter shake from the force of the abruptly-released energy. The sound was synthesized, not real, and coming from his dash speakers. Ethan saw his lasers make a direct hit and tear off a flaming chunk of the blocky twin-hulled fighter he was tracking. The enemy immediately went evasive and broke out of its attack pattern.

"Thanks for the save, Skidmark," Guardian Four said. It took Ethan a moment to realize she was talking to him. "Guess you're not such a dumb kakard after all."

Ethan smiled and stomped on the port rudder to bring the next enemy into line under his targeting reticle, but it turned to face him before he could get a laser lock. A second later it spat a stream of bright golden ripper fire at him. The first few shells splashed off his canopy shields with a sound like water hissing off a hot plate, jumping his aim and shaking his fighter. Ethan tried to reacquire his target, but before he'd lined up again, a warning siren sounded in his cockpit, and he noticed that his front shields were dangerously depleted.

Ethan stomped on the rudder and pushed his flight stick down, going evasive. He heard a few *thunks* as ripper shells glanced off his armor, and a computerized voice sounded with, "Front shields depleted."

Ethan gritted his teeth as he pulled through a high-G turn.

The gauge which showed him the state of his shields began flashing on the HUD, drawing his attention. What looked like four colored parentheses were arrayed around a 2D representation of his ship and flanked by glowing percentages.

Aft shields were blue—100%; front were red—slowly recovering at 2%; and both sides were in the green at just over 90%. A word flashed beneath the shield display—*equalize*—Ethan tried speaking the command aloud. "Equalize shields."

Gradually, he saw all four parentheses turn green. Another burst of ripper fire slammed into him, and his ship shuddered beneath the barrage. His aft shields immediately dropped into the red at 35%, and Ethan began jinking his fighter in earnest, rolling to starboard, side-slipping to port, pulling up hard . . . but the enemy pilot stayed on his tail through all the maneuvers, still appearing dead center behind him on the gravidar.

"I could use some help over here . . ." Ethan said.

"Roger that, I've got him, Skidmark." Three said. "Hang in there. . . ."

Ethan's ship shuddered again and his shields hissed with dissipating energy. An audible warning sounded: "Aft shields critical," and Ethan gritted his teeth, waiting for an explosion to rip into his back as his fighter was torn apart from behind.

Then his comm sounded with, "Missiles away! Fire your afterburners and get clear, Five!" That was from Guardian Three. Ethan struggled to find the switch for his afterburners. There were dozens of buttons whose functions were still a mystery to him. He'd only had time to figure out the basics of piloting a nova. It was a miracle he could even manage to target and shoot.

"Five, he's lining up above you to pull a switch over! I said get clear!"

"My afterburners are tapped out, Three!" Ethan lied in between decreasing his throttle and firing his starboard maneuvering jets in an attempt to slide out from under his opponent, but the pilot flying above him copied his maneuver exactly. Ethan felt panic seize his chest. The enemy pilot was going to bait and switch the missiles at the last minute, either by accelerating suddenly or pulling sharply away. Ethan grimaced. "I can't shake him!"

"Frek it!" Three said, and Ethan heard dymium lasers screeching out over the comm. A second later, a vicious explosion rocked his fighter. Bits of flaming wreckage rained down all around him. One hit his canopy with a sizzling *thunk* that knocked his forward shields down to 10% and elicited another critical shields alert from his ship's computer. Ethan quickly jammed his throttles to the max, jetting out from under the expanding debris cloud before something else could hit him. "Problem solved, Skidmark. I just shot down the hailfires before they reached the target. Lucky his shields were already weakened. The other two are making a break for it. Let them go. They're not worth the fuel and munitions. We'll hold ground here until the sentinels arrive to capture their base."

"I can't believe they were hiding this close to us, right under our noses!" Gina, Guardian Four, said. "They must have taken down the comm relay as a prelude to an attack on one of our convoys."

"Most likely," Three replied.

According to Ethan's file, Brondi's gang had knocked out the relay in order to give him an excuse to return to the Valiant and make his mission report in person.

"Form up, Guardians," Three said. "Staggered V formation."

"Roger that," Ethan replied. He wasn't sure what a staggered V should look like, but he assumed the shape of the formation was more or less what was implied. He brought his fighter into line behind Gina's nova and accelerated until he was flying parallel to her, and then the pair of them pulled up on Three's tail.

"Adan, weren't you supposed to meet up with Guardian Six before heading back to the *Valiant*?" A quick look at the comm display told Ethan it was Guardian Three who'd asked.

"He got delayed on Forliss Station," Ethan said. The truth was he was dead, just like Adan. The two of them had been out investigating a nova pilot's murder and they had quickly becomes victims of the killer themselves. "He had a problem with his fuel lines," Ethan went on. "He said he'd catch up with me once it was fixed."

"Damn fighters are always seizing up on us," Three said. "Well, let's hope nobody picks him off while he's on his own out there. Nova pilots are becoming common targets these days. Seems like we're everybody's enemy and nobody's friend."

"Guess they don't appreciate that we're out there every day risking our lives for them," Gina snorted.

"Guess not, but who's there to see it?" Three said.

Ethan frowned. He wasn't sure what they were talking about. The fleet hardly ever saw any action. Why were they talking about risking their lives? "There been much action while I was gone?"

"Not much aside from these pirates. It's a nice break from the real action, but no one stays here long before old Dominic sends us out on another scavenger hunt.

Ethan felt like he was missing something important. *Scavenger hunt?* "The last hunt find anything special?"

"Well, we won't know until they come back through the gate, but I'm sure it'll just be more of the same—survivors, equipment, ships."

The pieces of the puzzle began to gel in Ethan's brain— *survivors, equipment, and ships coming back through the gate?*

Realization dawned, and suddenly Ethan's eyes lost focus on the roiling red nebula around them.

"Five, tighten up, you're drifting!"

"Sorry ... got distracted," Ethan replied. He couldn't believe it! The overlord had reopened the gate, and he was sending hunting parties to go scouring the ruins of the ISS on the other side of the galaxy—the Sythian-infested side. It would only be a matter of time before someone got careless and was followed back to Dark Space. The overlord was putting them all at risk! Suddenly, Brondi's scheme to wipe out the fleet looked like a necessary evil.

Chapter 8

The sentinels came, landed on the asteroid where the pirates had made their base, and spent an hour clearing it to retrieve all the useful equipment before setting charges and blowing it to space dust. After that, they all jetted through the Chorlis-Firean gate and left the Firebelt Nebula behind.

Now, Ethan watched as the timer to real space counted down on his nav. As soon as it hit zero, the bright streaks and star lines of SLS faded to black, and Ethan saw the mottled white and blue ice world of Firea in the distance. Orbiting high above that, lying directly in front of the gate, was the *Valiant*—a massive, five-kilometer-long gladiator-class carrier. It was the largest surviving warship of the fleet, and the sole guardian of the Dark Space gate, since the other smaller cruisers and destroyers of the ISSF were scattered around Dark Space on patrol. The *Valiant* also carried a pair of 280-meter-long venture-class cruisers which had at the start of the Sythian War been the mainstay of the Imperial Fleet. There had once been more than a thousand of them, but now there were only five.

The *Valiant* glittered darkly against the icy night side of Firea. The carrier's reinforced, high-refraction index duranium hull caught and reflected the first rays of the system's red sun as it peeked feebly over the dawning edge of Firea. The planet's rocky moon lay as a dark silhouette behind the *Valiant*, and to one side of that, was the Dark Space gate, supposedly deactivated and sealed.

Ethan pressed his lips into a thin, determined line as he stared at the *Valiant*. This was his target. Somehow, he had to destroy that carrier. If not to serve Brondi's ends, then to keep the rest of Dark Space safe from Overlord Dominic's reaching. The overlord was sending ships through the gate! Surely he had to know the danger of that. They wouldn't even know if they were followed. Sythians had used cloaking devices to sneak their warships through the space gates before, and they would do it again.

"Tighten up, Five. . . ." Guardian Three said. He was beginning to get on Ethan's nerves. Ethan wasn't used to flying in formations, true, but did the man have to pick on him every time he wandered a few meters out of line?

Ethan clicked his comms as a trite way of acknowledging the order, and then he adjusted his nova's heading by a few degrees in order to appease his flight leader. A quick look at the interrogation file Brondi had given him revealed that Guardian Three was First Lieutenant Ithicus "Firestarter" Adari. The man was characterized as a rigid, by the book pilot with a wicked temper and a habit for picking fights that had earned him his call sign.

They drew near the amidships hangar of the *Valiant*, and soon the carrier began to loom over them, blocking out Ethan's view of everything else. He picked out a small speck flying alongside the carrier, near one of its yawning ventral hangar bays, and a second later Ethan realized that the speck was actually one of the carrier's two, 280-meter-long venture-class cruisers. The *Valiant* utterly dwarfed the cruiser.

Ethan shook his head in awe. Finer details began to emerge

all over the carrier's hull. The *Valiant* bristled with beam cannons and pulse lasers, as well as a few small and medium-caliber ripper turrets which functioned as the ship's AMS (Anti Missile System).

As they approached the carrier's hangar, Ethan was given a sense of the hangar's size by the seemingly endless fields of nova fighters and interceptors landed inside. They throttled back and passed through the static shields with a soft sizzle of exchanging energy. The static shields were weak atmospheric shields which created a pressure barrier strong enough to keep air locked inside, while still allowing ships to pass through without taking damage. During a battle those shields could be bolstered with the heavier beam and pulse shields to prevent enemy ships and missiles from flying into the hangar. Under those circumstances the novas were rather loaded into the rail launchers and then fired out at high speed to give them an evasive edge when flying into hot zones. Recovering the novas while under fire was a more complicated maneuver, however, which required precise timing on the part of both fighter pilots and hangar shield operators.

Ethan watched the hangar deck below milling with ground crew as the carrier's autopilot guided his fighter to an empty berth. Ground crew were bustling around the landed fighters, performing routine maintenance, and in some cases major repairs. Ethan frowned, confused by what he saw below. He'd been under the impression that the fleet was running out of fighters, but here, in just one of the carrier's six hangars, there was at least a full wing—six squadrons—which was considerably more than the reported two squadrons that were supposedly on active duty at the Dark Space gate. Either they were being lied to, or these were all of the grounded fighters that weren't fit for use anymore.

Ethan considered that he should probably take it for granted that they were being lied to. After all, the overlord was ordering excursions beyond Dark Space into occupied Sythian territory, while telling everyone that the gate was safely sealed.

Ethan's nova fighter settled down with a *thud-unk* on the deck beside a heavily-carbon-scored interceptor which had deep furrows gouged out of its sides and a black, ragged hole where the canopy should have been. Ethan wasn't sure what had happened to that fighter, but it was a fair bet that the pilot hadn't survived.

Ethan pressed the canopy release and the transpiranium bubble rose slowly with a hiss of equalizing air pressure and pneumatic pistons. A cool breeze swept in from the hangar, bringing with it the acrid smell of reactor coolant, thruster grease, and laser gas. Ethan crawled out of the cramped cockpit and hopped over the side of his fighter. He heard magnetic clamps locking around the landing struts of his nova. Those clamps would keep his ship from sliding around in the event that artificial gravity should fail.

Ethan stood on deck looking around dumbly for a moment, listening to the sounds of multiple thrusters spinning up or cooling down, of ground crew hollering at one another over great distances, and of the hangar's PA system blaring with a message for a Lieutenant Briggs to report to the quartermaster's office.

While Ethan took all of that in, someone came up behind him and slapped him on the back. He turned around to find himself staring down at a medium-height woman with dark blonde hair and angry amber eyes. Her face was hard, but not unappealing.

"I guess I owe you a drink for saving my ass back there."

This had to be Gina, Ethan decided. "Don't mention it.

Where is Firestarter?" Ethan asked, trying to make Guardian Three's call sign sound natural to his ears, but nothing he said sounded natural to his ears. His vocal synthesizer was faithfully mimicking the voice of the dead nova pilot whose identity he had stolen.

"He's arguing with a flight mechanic about a jammed-up laser cannon. We'd better go. We're due for debriefing in the Lieutenant Commander's office."

Ethan nodded absently. "Lead the way."

Gina turned and wordlessly began winding a path through the endless rows of scorched and battered fighters. Ethan eyed each fighter with a frown as they walked past. "Guess we've been running into more opposition than I thought. Either that or someone's been playing with the *Valiant's* beam cannons again."

Gina turned and gave him a funny look. "These are salvage from the war, Adan; you know that."

Ethan nodded and tried not to meet her gaze. "Right, just trying to crack a joke, Gina."

She snorted. "Well, stick to your real forte. Jokes never were a part of your repertoire."

"So what's my real forte, then?"

Gina shot him a dry look. "Shooting and frekking everything that moves."

Ethan grinned wryly. "I'm not sure if that was meant to be a compliment, but thanks."

"Right, well since making conversation isn't a part of your aforementioned skill set, let's leave it at that."

"What did I ever do to you, Gina?" He asked. Ethan was curious about how things had ended between Adan and Gina.

Gina turned to him with patiently raised eyebrows. "Really? You're going to ask me that? You know damn well what happened."

Ethan shrugged. "We don't have to be enemies."

"We don't have to be friends either."

With that, Ethan decided to drop it. She was right. He wasn't here to make friends—quite the opposite.

They reached the far wall of the hangar bay and Gina preceded him into a waiting rail car. A handful of ground crew and pilots piled in with them, including Guardian Three, who walked up to Ethan with a smirk and said, "Looks like you're losing your touch, Adan."

The rail car started forward with a subtle jolt and quickly accelerated up to a blinding speed. The walls of the rail tunnel blurred by them with bright streaks of light from passing glow panels, and Adan watched as Gina keyed a destination into the holoscreen mounted beside the doors of the rail car. Passengers were busily taking seats along the sides of the car, and Ethan followed suit, sitting down beside Guardian Three. He strapped in and then spared his squad mate a quick grin—just as he imagined the cocky Adan Reese might do.

Ithicus Adari glared back at him. He was large and well-built like Ethan; he had short, thinning black hair that lay flat against his head and a slowly pulsing blue tattoo peeked out from under the left sleeve of his flight suit. Ithicus also had a haggard, well-lined face which Ethan estimated made the man about five years his junior—though Ethan had to remember that his holoskin was actually projecting the image of a twenty-one-year-old. Ithicus had a square jaw, a crooked nose, and an angry gleam in his honey brown eyes. The man was obviously mean-tempered and he'd had his nose broken at least once, which couldn't have been an easy feat for a man his size.

"Losing my touch?" Ethan repeated with an accompanying snort. "Not likely."

"You almost got nailed by friendly fire, and you kept drifting out of formation. You forget how to fly or something?"

Ethan gritted his teeth. He'd only had a couple hours in the cockpit of a nova, and he was still getting used to the controls—the sensitivity, the idiosyncrasies of his particular fighter, and the raw, barely-contained power of a high-performance fighter versus his old sluggish *Atton*. The difference with his transport was that every maneuver had had to be exaggerated, but with a nova, just the slightest twitch of the controls could send him into an end over end spin. It was definitely an adjustment. Of course, he couldn't say any of that.

Ethan shrugged. "Guess I'm just tired, brua." Brondi's dossier on Adan had contained a list of more juvenile vocabulary for Ethan to work into his regular speech. He hoped it didn't sound as strange to those who knew Adan as it sounded to him.

Guardian Three smirked and looked away.

An automated voice sounded inside the rail car. "Coming up on, *Pilots' Center*."

Gina rose from her seat to grab hold of one of the vertical bars which ran down the center of the rail car. Ithicus rose, too, and Ethan groaned as he levered himself out of his chair. His muscles were cramping from having been cooped up in a nova cockpit for so long.

Gina looked him up and down and smiled. "You all right there, old timer?"

"Just fine, thanks."

The rail car slowed to a stop, and Ithicus nodded to the doors. "Let's go."

They spilled out into a broad corridor with subdued blue and white glow panels and shiny gray and black walls. Broad silver and gray pipes were tucked up against the ceiling and running down the center of the corridor. These were electrical conduits, water, sewage, and air ducts. Aboard fleet ships no one bothered to hide things away for aesthetics' sake.

The corridor was for the most part deserted, except for a janitor bot up ahead, polishing the floors with a monotonous *whirring* sound. They passed countless bulkheads and doors, all of which were labeled with black plates that glowed with bright blue descriptions: numbered simulator rooms, the officers' mess, a rec hall called "The Basement," which was roaring with a muffled ruckus from the men and women inside, and then came training rooms and lecture halls, followed by offices labeled with the names and ranks of various commanders to whom they belonged. The transpiranium panels in the doors of those offices and training rooms were all dark, all but one, whose golden light spilled weakly into the corridor. It was here that Guardian Three led them. The glowing door sign read, *Lieutenant Commander Rangel*. Guardian Three stopped to rap smartly on the door, and it opened automatically to let them in.

They piled into the small office beyond the door and stepped up to a shiny white desk as the door swished shut behind them. Sitting behind that desk was a small man with an angular face and an intense blue gaze. Absent from that gaze was the usual spark of warmth which betrayed a person's humanity. He was clothed in the typical black with white trim uniform of the fleet. The rank insignia on the upper left sleeve of his uniform was the characteristic gold chevron of a lieutenant commander with a silver nova fighter in the middle. Behind the commander was a broad viewport which showed a dawning blue-white slice of the planet Firea far below.

Guardian Three, Ithicus Adari, stopped in front of the commander's desk and saluted. Ethan and Gina gave their own salutes, to which the commander nodded and said, "At ease. Report."

Ithicus spoke first: "Four pirates jumped us at the Chorlis-Firean gate while we were waiting for repair crews to check out the gate's comm relay. The array was riddled with holes from ripper cannons. The pirates were armed with the same. It's a fair bet they took out the array. The pirates had established a temporary base on one of the asteroids in the Firebelt Nebula, no doubt to stand by and wait for one of our convoys. They must have taken out the comm array so we'd be deaf to hear any distress calls. Adan joined us at the start of the fight, and we managed to destroy two of the enemy fighters and clip another one before they ran. The pirates' base was rudimentary, but sentinels recovered a small amount of useful equipment and supplies before demolishing it."

The commander frowned and began rubbing his chin thoughtfully. "Good. Any signs of the pirates' affiliation?"

Ithicus shook his head. "They covered their tracks well."

"Hmmm. We'll have investigators look over the confiscated material for clues. Dismissed," the commander said with a wave of his hand. They began turning to leave, but Vance shook his head and pointed at Ethan. "Not you." Ethan stopped and turned back to the commander's desk.

Once the others had left, the commander raised his eyebrows and leaned forward. Taking that as his cue, Ethan spoke up. "I was on my way back to the *Valiant* when I stumbled on Guardians Three and Four. They were already under attack, so I joined the fight. The rest is as Three already said."

The commander shook his head. "I'm not interested in any of that. I want to know what happened to your mission and why you're back here without your wingman."

"My mission was a fair success, sir."

The commander's ice blue eyes narrowed. "So you tracked down Lieutenant Gerbrand's killer?"

"Yes, sir."

"And he's dead?"

"Not exactly. The killer is a bounty hunter named Verlin."

The commander waved his hand impatiently. "One of many aliases. I already know that; we sent you on this mission with that information. What else did you find out?"

"He's working for Brondi." That wasn't actually a part of Ethan's cover story, but it was true, and it would help maintain his cover better than the lame excuse he'd been given. Moreover, he gained some small personal satisfaction from selling Brondi down the river.

"Brondi, hmmm? Not too surprising. Well, then what are you doing back so soon? Your mission isn't over."

"I was unable to pursue the bounty hunter further. He retreated aboard Alec Brondi's corvette, and I felt it would be better not to follow him without backup. I tried to comm the *Valiant* for further orders, but the comms weren't getting through." Ethan went on, "When I realized the commnet must be down, I went back to the rendezvous with Six, but his fuel lines were jammed, so I left him on Forliss Station to make repairs while I came back here to refuel and report." In reality, Six was also dead, also killed by Verlin.

"Interesting." Vance steepled his fingers under his chin, and his angular features grew even more vulturine as he contemplated the news. "Well, I'll file your report, and we'll see what command has to say, but if all of that is true, and Brondi has taken to openly opposing the fleet, he's going to be in for more trouble than he's bargained for."

"Yes, sir. May I be dismissed now, Commander?"

"Of course. You sound like you could use some downtime. Your voice is a little strange."

"Strange, sir?" Ethan asked.

Vance nodded. "Like you're hoarse. You sure you're not coming down with something?"

Ethan hesitated before shaking his head. "Not that I'm aware of, sir. I must just be tired."

"Well, barring any emergencies, I'm taking you off active duty until Six returns with his report, so go get some rest. We don't need you making the other pilots sick. Dismissed."

Ethan nodded and turned to leave the commander's office. He let out a long sigh as the door swished shut behind him. *Damn you, Brondi, with all your millions of sols, you couldn't afford to get me a better vocal synthesizer? My voice is a little strange? That can't be good.* He would just have to speak as little as possible until his mission was over.

Ethan walked down the corridor to the rail car tunnel at the end, punched the summon car button, and waited for the next car to arrive. He needed to retreat to his quarters for a vaccucleanse and to formulate a plan to sabotage the *Valiant*. Ethan watched as the control panel beside the doors to the rail tunnel ticked down the ETA for the next car. After a moment of idle contemplation, he realized that he didn't even know where his quarters were, so he pulled the mission data card Brondi had given him out of his pocket and slotted it into the input just behind his right ear to examine the contents of the card more privately than a holo reader would allow. That implant had come in handy over the years. It was essentially a small computer which fed data straight to his brain.

As he searched the document, Ethan heard someone shout out behind him, "Hey, Skidmark, aren't you going to let me buy you that drink?"

Ethan mentally closed his link to the data card and turned to face Gina. She walked up to him with a sarcastic smile. "I like to pay my debts. Who knows, maybe I'll even give you tips to help you lure some unsuspecting sclut to your quarters for the night."

"Really? You'd do that for me? I'm touched, Gina."

Her expression became exasperated and she stopped a half a dozen feet away from him. "No, you depraved pervert. Just a drink. Come on." Not bothering to insist further, she turned on her heel and walked back the way she'd come.

Ethan hesitated, considering her offer for a moment before deciding to follow her. He broke into a light jog to catch up, and then he flashed Gina a winning smile. She rolled her eyes and looked away.

He supposed it couldn't hurt to mingle a bit. After all, he'd need to gather some information about the *Valiant* in order to properly sabotage it. The people to talk to in order to glean that information would almost certainly be pilots and engineers, all of whom he would find inside the ship's rec halls.

They reached the rec hall they'd passed earlier called "The Basement," and Ethan stepped up to the control panel to key the door open. The door swished aside to reveal a large, darkly-lit room with a ceiling full of uncovered pipes. The walls were filled with floor to ceiling holoscreens and dark gray furniture was arrayed before them. Small knots of pilots were lounging there, drinking and playing games. A long, elliptical bar counter stood in the center of the room, and on the other side of that, Ethan glimpsed a padded arena where a group of pilots were busy battling each other with small, remote-controlled assault mechs while dozens of others looked on and cheered for their favorites to win. Ethan followed Gina up to the bar, and they sat down together.

Gina raised a hand to call the bartender over. "Egrit!" The bartender turned and nodded to her. He was a scary-looking man with a bald head, multiple glowing blue and red tattoos on his arms and face, and a few spiky subcutaneous piercings in his knuckles. Ethan felt like he'd met a dozen men just like Egrit during his time on Etaris.

"Yea?" Egrit asked.

"Two black mavericks," Gina said, and offered her upturned wrist to the man. He grabbed her wrist none too gently and passed a wand over it before turning to a cooler behind him and pulling out two frosty transpiranium bottles filled with bubbling black beer. Black mavericks were brewed from heavily fermented Forlissan Black Grass and Chorlisean Wheat. The result was a meal in a bottle that could knock you out cold if you weren't used to it. Ethan wondered that they were even allowed to serve such potent drinks to pilots, but he supposed that they weren't on the active duty roster, so it didn't matter much.

Gina raised her beer and held it out to Ethan for a toast. "To another day among the living."

Ethan raised his own beer and clinked his bottle with hers. "To not being dead," he replied and took a sip of his Maverick. He reveled in the strong, bittersweet flavor of the beer. It had been a long time since he'd had the sols to afford more than water. When he set his beer down, he noticed that Gina hadn't taken a sip of hers yet. She was frozen with the bottle halfway to her lips, staring at him with eyebrows raised and a look of utter perplexity on her face.

"What?" Ethan asked.

She nodded to his left hand which was still clamped around his bottle of beer. "Since when do you wear a wedding ring, Adan?"

Chapter 9

Ethan couldn't believe he'd been stupid enough to put his wedding ring back on after the holo suit. It was an old habit by now for him to wear the ring. He'd always considered it a kind of good luck charm, but now it was about to get him into a lot of trouble.

"Wedding ring?" he echoed. "Is that what this is?" He made a show of examining the simple silver band on his left ring finger.

"Yes, Adan, that's exactly what it is. Don't tell me you didn't know. What, are you hoping that women will prefer a married man?" Gina shook her head. "That's twisted, even for you, Skidmark. Where did you even *find* that? Rare to see a wedding band at all these days."

Ethan decided to stick with naïveté as an excuse. "An old storekeeper on Forliss Station sold it to me. He said it would bring me luck."

Gina snorted and narrowed her eyes. "And since when did you become superstitious?"

Another wrong move. Ethan turned to her with what he hoped to be a disarming smile. "Hey, what's with the interrogation? I thought you just wanted to buy me a drink. It's beginning to sound suspiciously like you want to get to know me better. Maybe you had an ulterior motive for offering that drink. Hoping to get into my pants, are we? All you have to do is ask, Gina."

That did it. Ethan watched Gina's expression turn from curious to furious in a matter of seconds. "You know what, you're right." She rose from her bar stool, taking her beer with her. "Enjoy your drink, Adan." With that, she turned and stormed off, leaving him alone at the bar.

Ethan took another sip of his black maverick and caught a nasty grin from Egrit. "Someone's not getting any tonight," the bartender said, chuckling.

Ethan was about to reply that he wasn't looking for any action, but then he remembered he had to stay in character, so he cocked his head and gave a haughty smile. "Don't be too sure about that. I'll have who I want, when I want, and how I want them—two or three at a time if it suits me. I don't have to ask nicely, because they're already begging."

Egrit burst into gruff laughter. "Same old Skidmark!" He turned away, shaking his head, and Ethan smiled. It seemed like he'd managed to nail down Adan's character perfectly. The boy had obviously been insufferably arrogant and rude with everyone around him. If he'd had redeeming qualities, Ethan wasn't sure what they might be.

Taking advantage of the peace and quiet, Ethan mentally pulled up his dossier again and searched for directions to Adan's quarters aboard the *Valiant*. After a few minutes, he realized that there was no mention anywhere in the file of where Adan stayed. Ethan frowned. If he wanted to rest and get cleaned up, he was going to have to *ask* someone where his quarters were—and wouldn't *that* be a dead giveaway. Or, he could just get horribly drunk and feign amnesia. . . . Why not? He'd be buying drinks on Adan's tab. At least that way he'd get something back for the pain of extracting his identichip and implanting Adan's in its place.

Ethan signaled to Egrit, who was busy serving an attractive looking woman at the other end of the bar counter. She caught his eye and smiled. Ethan was taken aback by that and rather than returning her smile, he looked away, embarrassed.

Then he remembered who he was supposed to be and he chided himself for responding so out of character, but it was too late. He tried for the bartender's attention again, and this time he succeeded. Egrit walked up to him, and asked, "Yea?"

Ethan nodded to his beer and offered his wrist to Egrit. "Keep them—" He suddenly broke into a fit of coughing as his throat began tickling maddeningly. He shook his head. "Sorry," he said, his voice sounding hoarse now even to his ears. "Throat must be dry. Keep them coming," he said, tapping the side of his beer.

The bartender frowned at him. "You don't sound too good, Lieutenant. Maybe you should go get some rest."

"No, I'm fine. Get me another drink and I'll be even better."

Egrit snorted. "Whatever you say, Skidmark."

* * *

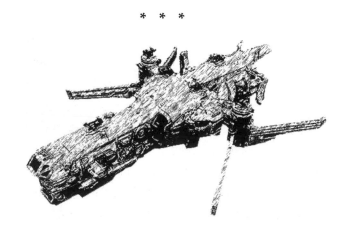

Alara watched Brondi offer her that gaping smile of his. "Either you're planning to eat me, or you're happy to see me," Alara said as she walked up to the cell door.

"So charming," Brondi said from the other side. "Your talents are being wasted in here, Sweet Thing. I could have you making more sols per hour than most people make in a week. What do you say? I'll even let you have your pick of which of my pleasure palaces you'd like to work in."

Alara found her hands closing in white-knuckled fists around the bars of her cell. "You'd have to implant me with a slave chip before I'd ever agree to that."

Brondi cocked his head suddenly to one side, as though he'd just had an epiphany. "Why, that is a novel idea! I do believe I'll take your advice, thank you."

Alara felt dread and horror welling up inside of her, threatening to burst forth in a scream, but she clamped down on it, unwilling to give Brondi the satisfaction. Instead, she just glared at his loathsome, pudgy face, willing his head to explode. "What about Ethan's bargain? I thought you were going to release us once he got your information for you."

"Oh, yes, Ethan! About him . . ." Brondi's grin turned even nastier and his wild, bloodshot gray eyes sparkled madly. "He's not coming back, Sweet Thing."

Alara's face became stricken. "What do you mean?"

"Well, you see the story Ethan gave you was not entirely true. I *did* send him to sabotage the *Valiant* so I could be rid of the fleet's perpetual meddling in my affairs, but . . . that was never going to work." Brondi shook his head sadly.

"Ethan would never agree to do that."

"Actually," Brondi said, raising a finger to silence her objections, "he did, but it doesn't matter. Not even Ethan knows what he's really doing aboard the *Valiant*, and it'll be too late by the time he figures it out. Right now your boy toy is a walking time bomb, just waiting to explode."

"What you mean?" Alara demanded. She rattled the bars of her cell, and Brondi's mouth gaped in another smile.

"Feisty! That's going to come in handy in your new profession."

"What have you done to Ethan?"

Brondi shook his head sadly. "The better question is, what am I about to do to you?" Brondi gestured to someone just out of her line of sight, and a pair of men came into view. One of them held a wicked-looking chip implanter, while the other held a stun pistol—and he was aiming it at her.

"Say goodbye, Alara. When you wake up, you'll be going by Angel."

Alara opened her mouth to scream, and she turned to run, but there was nowhere to go. The stun bolt hit her in the back with an electrifying jolt, and her muscles went to jelly. Before she even hit the floor, everything faded to black.

Chapter 10

As Ethan was ordering his third maverick, a group of half-drunk pilots strolled up to him at the bar. One of them pulled out the bar stool next to him and hopped up. Ethan spared him a grumpy look. It was Ithicus Adari, Guardian Three. The others stayed back, whispering and shushing each other, standing there looking stupid with knowing grins pasted on their faces. Among them was Gina. Their eyes met briefly, and Ethan saw that hers were glittering with something dark and ugly. Ithicus draped an arm over his shoulder and said, "Hoi there, Skidmark."

"Hoi brua," Ethan said drily.

"Don't suppose you'd like to join us for a short sim run."

"Mmmm, I'm tired. I think I'll just stay here."

"Let's make it interesting," Ithicus said, ignoring him. "Sythians versus the ISSF. How about . . . the Rokan Defense. You command the ISSF and I'll command the Sythians. You say you're a 5A rating and you have a natural instinct for command—" A few snorts of laughter erupted from the group of pilots standing behind Ethan, and Ithicus shrugged his big shoulders. "Well, here's your chance to prove it, Skidmark. You'll have an advantage that the Rokans didn't. You'll know that the invasion is coming."

Ethan slowly turned to look at Ithicus. There was a sarcastic gleam in his dark eyes which told Ethan he was being mocked somehow and that Ithicus didn't actually expect him to accept the offer, but Ethan *was* actually interested. He'd never witnessed any of the battles with the Sythians, and Roka IV had been his home. He wanted to see if at least one of the millions of massacres visited upon humanity by the alien invaders could have been prevented. Making the offer even more tempting, Ethan actually did have a 5A rating, and he was tired of people telling him that it was a fake. Maybe Adan's had been, but Ethan had earned his rating back in the Rokan Academy, not from an unscrupulous vendor in Dark Space.

"Okay." Ethan nodded. "Let's do it."

Ithicus's grin flickered, surprise showing through. Obviously the whole thing had been a bluff to somehow irritate Adan Reese, but Ethan was not Adan. Ithicus recovered smoothly and his expression became smirking. "Want to make it interesting?"

Ethan frowned. He wasn't sure what he was getting into, so betting on the outcome was a bad idea, but what did he really have to lose, anyway? "What do you have in mind?"

"If you beat me, I'll switch places with you on your next rotation. You can stay in Dark Space on patrol, while I go to the frontlines. If you lose, you take a double shift out there and I take *your* patrol duty."

Ethan's brow furrowed. *The frontlines?* he wondered. *What frontlines?* "Ah ... sure, but you have to give me odds. Everyone knows the Rokan Defense was an impossible fight to win." Ethan didn't actually know that, but it was a fair bet. He didn't know anything about what had happened on Roka IV. He'd been mining for dymium on Etaris at the time, and he'd only heard about his world falling to the invaders after the ruins there were already cold.

Ithicus nodded. "That goes without saying, Skidmark. No one *wins* the Rokan Defense. You just have to beat my command and tactical ratings from my last run through the mission as the ISSF."

Ethan swirled the last of his black maverick around in the bottom of the bottle, contemplating the black depths of the beer before downing it in one last swig.

"What do you say?" Ithicus pressed.

Ethan set his bottle down with a *thunk* and turned to his squad mate with a thin-lipped smile. "You got yourself a bet, brua, but you're going to regret it."

Ithicus matched Ethan's smile. "We'll see about that."

* * *

All of a 20 minutes later Ethan was standing on the simulated bridge of a venture-class cruiser. He'd taken a few minutes while the simulator's holo field was energizing to review a few of the comments and mission reports made by other pilots in order to properly familiarize himself with the mission, and now he felt at least reasonably confident that he could make a good accounting for himself—whether or not he'd beat Ithicus Adari's scores was another matter.

Ethan looked around the bridge. He was surrounded by other officers, some real, and some AIs. Before him lay the captain's table, a holo table standing on a raised walkway that ran between the half a dozen different control stations on the bridge—three to his left and three to his right. Those control stations fed the captain's table with a continuous stream of data, and there, overlaid on a glowing blue grid, Ethan was given an overview of the Rokan system and the forces under his command. Ethan spun in a slow circle on the deck, nodding to a few of his bridge crew as they stared expectantly at him.

All of this was intensely familiar. It evoked strong memories from his childhood, back when his only cares in the world had been his grades in school and girls. Back then, when he'd had something called "free time" he'd spent it hanging out at Roka City's sim center with his friends, running and re-running simulated fleet actions, which were of course all pure fiction—the real ones were classified. Those missions had been created for the solitary purpose of entertainment. Ethan had been the commander of a venture-class cruiser on more than one occasion, and although the recreational sims did appear to have some distinct differences from this one, most of what he saw around him on the bridge was the same.

Ethan walked up to the captain's table and ran a hand along the smooth black border of the glowing blue grid. This was the whole reason he'd become a pilot, and the whole reason he had a 5A rating today. He'd earned his 5A rating in sims long before he'd ever had a chance to earn it for real. Back then he'd had big plans for his life; on more than one occasion he'd imagined himself becoming a fleet admiral, commanding an entire flotilla of ISSF warships. That was before hard times had hit—before his mother had become sick. At age 17 he'd been faced with the choice of dropping out of school to get a job or watching them both starve, which wasn't really a choice at all. Once he'd dropped out, there was no going back. No fleet recruiter would take a high school dropout—not back then, anyway.

At first he'd just run the odd courier mission, flying a small flitter around Roka City—no questions asked. He never got to see the cargo, which always fit into a small black carrying case, but he was strictly warned to stay away from authorities. His cover had been that he was a rich young man, spoiled to excess, and just out joyriding, looking for girls to pick up. He'd never been searched, but there'd been a few close scrapes when he'd had to lose pursuing patrollers in the winding canyons and multi-leveled streets of Roka City. Once his employment agency realized what a good pilot he was, they had him running interstellar hops. Before he knew it, he was making enough money to pay for more than just food; he was paying for his mother's expensive medical treatments and making it look like she was cashing in on a pension she didn't know she'd had. He'd even had enough money left over after all of that to store up a significant rainy day fund, which had eventually been what he'd used to buy his house with Destra, to make a life for them and Atton. He'd had a good run like that, smuggling stims for over two decades before he'd finally been caught.

And now, now all of that seemed like a dream—like those memories belonged to someone else's life, not his. Ethan began absently studying the grid, forcing himself back to the here and now. He had a bet to win.

At his disposal he had four cruisers, including his own, six destroyers, and dozens of nova squadrons, all of them spread out and combing the system with active sensors for an invisible enemy, but space was too vast to pick up the muted signatures of heavily cloaked Sythian vessels, and Ethan had read the mission reports from the other pilots who'd gone through the sim before him—no patrols had ever found Sythian ships before they'd wanted to be found. Also from the mission notes Ethan knew which way the Sythians were coming from, and when, but he had just a few minutes to gather his forces into a unified front before the Sythians would strike, and gathering his fleet in that time would be impossible at relativistic speeds.

"Comms, have our vessels make short SLS jumps to the following coordinates. . . ."

The XO interrupted him before he could speak. "What about our fighters?"

Ethan shook his head. "No time to collect them. We'll have to do without them for a while."

His XO snorted. "A while? The battle will be over by the time they get here. It would be better to go evasive now and fall back to Roka while the other ships collect their novas."

Ethan ignored the advice. "*Falconian* to 9-4-9." He waited a beat for the comm officer to relay the command. "*Borealis* to 9-4-4." Again he waited while the comm officer spoke softly into his headset. "*Tretina* to 4-4-4." Those were his other three cruisers. He also had half a dozen guardian-class destroyers to collect. "Make the destroyers line up at 10-4-1, 10-4-2, 10-4-3, and so on."

The comm officer went on relaying the orders into his headset, and Ethan turned the other way, to his chief engineer. "Set our shields to maximum, all front and sides, and increase weapons power. Rob engines to do so and set shipboard systems to emergency power only."

The engineer nodded. "Yes, sir."

"Helm, kill thrust."

"*Kill* thrust, sir?"

"Yes, we're not going to outmaneuver an enemy we can't see."

"Yes, sir."

Ethan caught a look from his XO. "Traditionally commanders have done well to keep engines powered," she said. "The Sythians have a hard time keeping up with their slower drives, and their weapons have a shorter range than ours."

"True, but until we know where they are, we can't be sure we won't be running straight into a trap." That was another thing Ethan had gleaned from the previous pilots' mission reports. "They need their cloaking devices to get close to us, and I'm not going to help them do that faster by roaring around blindly at full speed."

"Hmmm," Ethan's XO said, but she left it at that. He didn't recognize the blonde-haired woman who was his second-in-command, but from the gold chevron on her sleeve and the silver icon of a venture-class emblazoned over it, he realized that she was a Deck Commander, and that meant she outranked him by a considerable margin. For the purposes of this mission, however, Ethan was in command. He turned away from her to address his gunnery chief. "Guns, have all of our pulse lasers and beams standing by. On my mark I want them to begin a firing pattern on low power. Have them fire a volley every five seconds, staggered. I want them firing in all directions at once. Don't hit our own, but make sure they each sweep their guns to cover a fifteen degree arc. Paint three overlapping circles of fire around us, and keep those circles moving so we cover as much of space as possible. We're sounding out the enemy, so have them on the lookout for any direct hits, lasers and beams abruptly disappearing into nothingness, bits of debris flying out of deep space—that sort of thing. The minute any one of them sees something strange, have them flag it on the grid."

"Yes, sir," the weapons officer said.

Ethan could sense his XO glaring at him again, so he turned to face her with a patient smile. "Yes, Deck Commander Caldin?"

"We'll run flat out of energy before the enemy even gets here. What's more, they'll see us shooting and simply stay back out of range until we're spent. By the time we're out of charge they'll swoop in and de-cloak all around us, blasting us to bits while our guns are still recharging. We won't have a single joule of laser energy left to shoot them with."

"We'll still have our warheads."

"They'll shoot them down! You can't rely on warheads. Sythian ships have better point defenses than we do, and their gunners are more accurate by far."

"Trust me, commander, and remember who is charge of this mission."

Loba Caldin looked away with a scowl and out the forward viewports.

Ethan waited, watching the countdown he'd set up on his captain's table. The Sythians were due to attack in less than one minute. He watched as his ships began winking off the grid as they jumped to SLS. Ethan bided his time, hoping his gamble would pay off. Leaving his command vessel all alone, under no power, he felt sure that Ithicus wouldn't pass up the opportunity to take him out early. Once all of Ethan's other vessels were in SLS, and the timer he'd set up reached ten seconds, he turned and nodded to the gunnery chief. "Mark!"

And suddenly space around them was lit up with streams of red and blue laser fire. The deck began vibrating underfoot with the continuous release of energy.

Ethan watched keenly on the captain's table, waiting for the gunners to find and flag targets. He didn't have to wait long. Dozens of waypoints began appearing on the map all around them, marked by the gunners as possible enemy targets. A moment later, Ethan heard the gunnery chief report, "We have multiple contacts!"

Ethan nodded decisively. In that precise moment the rest of the fleet dropped out of SLS all around his cruiser, and he called out, "Transmit coordinates to our other vessels and tell them to concentrate fire, warheads only, set to detonate close to, but not right on top of the enemy targets! Have their laser batteries begin sounding out the enemy at the coordinates we've supplied, and keep our batteries firing in the existing pattern. Arm our missiles and stand by for my mark. Helm, full speed ahead."

Ethan looked up and out the forward viewports to see the first of his cruisers, the *Falconian*, which lay just off their starboard side, opening up with a volley of dozens of streaking missiles and torpedoes. The first torpedo reached its designated coordinates almost immediately, and flared in a blinding starburst explosion. As that explosion faded, a second torpedo hit, adding to the first one's explosive punch, and then, even before the rest of the missiles had found their mark, there came an enormous secondary explosion, and the large flaming bulk of an enemy ship appeared out of nowhere, slowly cracking in half. The rest of the warheads streaked in and exploded just behind the first two, chipping away at the doomed vessel's thruster banks.

"One down!" Ethan roared, and the bridge erupted with an abbreviated cheer. Suddenly the deck rocked underfoot and their shields hissed noisily as enemy fire found them. Ethan's gaze shot back to the captain's table to see more than a hundred enemy signatures appearing all around them.

"Evasive action!" Ethan ordered. "All guns target the nearest enemy!" The ship rocked with an explosion. "And equalize our shields! Have the fleet form up with us. We're getting out of here."

No wonder Roka had fallen. They were just ten against a hundred plus. The enemy ships were unshielded, their drives were slower, and their weapons were shorter ranged, but their hulls were still hard enough to crack that Ethan didn't think he stood much of a chance. He was facing an entire armada, not a fleet. Ethan noted the flaming wrecks which had appeared all around them—nine in all—which were the result of his initial sounding for the enemy. Nine of the enemy cruisers had been taken out before the enemy had even managed to fire a single shot. Ethan grinned. It had been a logical maneuver, since the Sythians couldn't fire while they were cloaked—due to some sort of energy trade-off—and they took just long enough to de-cloak that the missiles had all found their targets before enemy point defenses could come online to take them out.

Space spun around them as the helm tried to evade enemy fire, and Ethan watched out the forward viewports as hundreds of blinding purple stars shot out from the nearest enemy cruiser and rushed at them in spiraling arcs. These were the Sythian warheads, their preferred weapon for all occasions—tracking packets of energy that were impossible to shoot down, and went off like a hailfire missile. A few dozen of them exploded in a fiery cloud on the bow of the cruiser and chipped off a flaming chunk of the ship. Ethan watched on the captain's table as another enemy cruiser winked off the grid behind them, and then his attention was drawn back to the forward viewports as a blinding blue flash of light shot out from their bow. Their batteries had switched focus to the enemy in front. Ethan watched bright blue beams draw flaming lines across the enemy cruiser's hull. Not more than a few seconds later the enemy ship fell silent and Ethan's gunners moved on to the next target.

"Port shields critical!" the engineering chief called out. "Equalizing."

"Get up to that wreck and use it as a shield!" Ethan pointed to the flaming derelict before them which was now venting fiery streams of atmosphere into space. They flew past the ragged remains of the enemy ship, close enough to see the shifting blue and lavender patterns on the gleaming hull. A stream of purple stars which had been meant for them slammed into the derelict and it erupted with even more gouts of flame. For the time being, however, the derelict was holding off enemy fire.

"Aft shields critical!"

Suddenly the deck rocked with an explosion, nearly knocking everyone off their feet or out of their control stations. That was the first warning that something was wrong with the inertial management system. Ethan felt the deck tilting dangerously under his feet.

The engineering officer called out: "IMS failing!" And that was Ethan's second warning.

Thinking fast, Ethan called out, "Helm, cease maneuvering!" But it was too late. The inertial management system failed, and everyone flew into the ceiling, following the path of their inertia. Ethan felt no pain from the impact, since it was only a simulation, but he saw the world around him fade to black as though he'd actually been knocked unconscious; then the simulator pod hissed open, and he was left blinking up at the glow panels in the ceiling of the simulator room. He lay there for a long moment, a sense of failure and helplessness washing over him. He'd been there, fighting for his home, and not only had he not he saved Roka, but he hadn't even managed to take out more than a small fraction of the enemy fleet. Ethan grimaced. He'd surely lost the bet with Ithicus—not that it mattered. He wasn't going to be around long enough for Ithicus to collect.

A moment later, a familiar face appeared above his pod, and Ethan found himself staring up at Deck Commander Caldin. She held out a hand to help him out of the pod. Once they were standing face to face, she nodded abruptly and smiled. "Good job, Adan."

Ethan blinked. "I'm sorry, what?"

"You did surprisingly well."

His eyes narrowed at that. Surely she was mocking him. "What's that supposed to mean?"

"Your mission was a complete success. You beat the high score, and you beat my own personal best by an order of magnitude."

"I did?"

She nodded. "What . . . how many ships did we take out?"

"Twenty in all. The previous record was four."

Ethan's eyes widened. "And you?"

"My record was two."

Ethan gaped. "Did the war always go so poorly for us?"

Caldin shook her head. "It generally went worse. The Sythians didn't have any territories to defend, and we couldn't track their movements. The result was that they roamed around in massive fleets like the one you just saw, and we couldn't optimize our defenses, so our own forces were always hopelessly outnumbered."

"We should have grouped together, sacrificed a few worlds to meet them on an even footing."

"We tried that, but they just kept hitting us wherever we weren't, and our worlds fell even faster."

Ethan grimaced. "Kavaar . . ."

"Don't worry. We're making a better accounting for ourselves now that the shoe's on the other foot and we've adapted their cloaking tech."

Ethan's eyes widened. That was the first he'd heard of cloaking devices aboard human ships. During the war, finding ways to adapt Sythian technology had been pure fantasy, but somehow since then they'd made significant advances in that department.

Ethan heard more pods hissing open all around the room and his attention was drawn off to watch as the rough dozen other pilots in the simulator room climbed out of their pods and started toward him and Loba Caldin. "So the war is going well now?" Ethan asked absently, his eyes settling on a red-faced Ithicus Adari.

The deck commander turned to watch, too, as the other pilots approached. "Quite well, yes, but you won't have to trouble yourself with that for some time. Seems like Firestarter is on his way to the frontlines instead of you. Pity though. We could use someone with your instincts out there." She turned back to him then. "And not in the cockpit of a nova, either. I'm going to recommend you for immediate promotion to a command position."

Ethan turned to meet her gaze with a frown. "The fleet has open command positions?"

"We're salvaging more and more ships every day." She shrugged. "Should my recommendation be accepted, and assuming you pass the tests laid out for you, you'll be in command of your own cruiser before you can blink."

Ethan blinked. "Well, I don't know what to say. . . ."

The others arrived then and began offering Ethan their congratulations, some of them genuine, others envious or suspicious—as though he'd somehow cheated.

"Don't say anything yet," Caldin replied, shouting to be heard above the ruckus. "But I'll be in touch."

Ethan nodded and turned to Ithicus who had stopped before him with an angry scowl. Ethan's eyes narrowed, but Ithicus thrust out his hand, and Ethan accepted the handshake warily.

"That was some stunt you pulled, Skidmark. Nice." And then Ithicus let go of his hand and walked off. Ethan watched him leave while enduring a steady stream of offers from the other pilots to buy him drinks in exchange for insight into his strategies. Ethan decided to take them up on it, and he followed them back to the bar. He didn't have anything better to do, and maybe one of them could help him find his quarters later, but as Ethan reached the doors to The Basement, he felt a crushing wave of fatigue come over him. His head began throbbing and he felt another maddening tickle start in the back of his throat. A moment later that tickle sent him into a fit of coughing which had the nearest pilot staring at him curiously.

"You all right, Skidmark?"

Ethan nodded as they walked inside the rec hall. "Yeah, brua. Throat's just a little dry from screaming orders, that's all."

The other pilot grinned. "Well, we'll fix that! Egrit!"

* * *

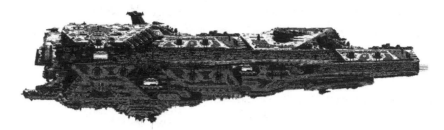

Supreme Overlord Altarian Dominic, commander in chief and head of state for the ISS—what was left of it anyway—sat in a vast, luxuriously-appointed room which served as his quarters aboard the *Valiant*. It was the middle of the night, but he couldn't sleep. He needed to steal a few hours for himself, even if he had to rob himself of sleep to do so. All day, every day, he was under constant scrutiny, constantly forced to uphold an image of himself that he didn't feel inside, but here, away from all the prying eyes, all of his pretenses were stripped away and he could finally relax and be himself. No one knew what that stripped-down version of him looked like, but that couldn't be helped. The overlord had a certain persona to maintain, a certain confidence and optimism to uphold—like he knew exactly what he was doing, and no matter what he would never fail.

Nothing could be further from the truth.

Dominic turned his big black chair toward the room's broad, floor-to-ceiling viewport, and he looked down upon the ice world of Firea far below. He studied the whorled blue and white patterns of the glaciers on the surface, and they brought to mind images from his youth on Roka IV. He remembered watching as a young child from the balcony of his home as the snow shivered down from the colossal mountains around Roka City—avalanches that were periodically triggered by the miners as they blasted for dymium with detlor charges.

That seemed like a lifetime ago. *I am quite old now, after all,* he thought with a wry twist of his lips. His hair was white, his features thoroughly wrinkled—these days when he looked in the mirror he didn't even recognize himself.

The overlord was saddled with the immense responsibility of safe-guarding the remnants of humanity, while still finding ways to strike back against the Sythians from the shadows of Dark Space. It was a responsibility which he often felt he was ill-suited to bear. He was too inexperienced to be an adequate commander, but everyone was looking to him with false hope, expecting him to have the experience necessary to guide them safely through these troubled times.

Dominic sighed and turned from the view of Firea back to his desk. There was a holoscreen there, dark and silent, just waiting for him to activate it and review the day's events and mission reports. This was where he monitored the state of the empire and made decisions with far-reaching consequences, sending orders to commanders which would seal their fates as well as those of the thousands of fleet officers serving under them.

Dominic waved his hand before the screen, gesturing for it to wake up. There were twenty five messages awaiting a reply. Opening his mail, Dominic scanned through the list, trying to find a place to start. One message in particular caught his attention—from Captain Storian, in charge of the command training program. Dominic opened the message and read the details. It was a letter of introduction for a nova pilot, Adan Reese, who Captain Storian recommended for immediate promotion and admittance to the command training program. Attached were the pilot's simulator scores from the Rokan Defense. He'd broken the previous records in that mission by a startling margin, using some very unconventional tactics to do so. Captain Storian went on to say that it was either a fluke or a sign of significant command potential, and it was worth finding out which.

Dominic found he was curious despite himself. He'd set up the command training program in the hopes of someday finding a commander worthy to replace him as commander in chief of the fleet. Could this pilot be such a man?

A quick look at Adan's identicard revealed he was too young to have much real experience, and the pilot's psychological evaluation further revealed he was ill-suited to command—arrogant, rude, impulsive, and selfish. Dominic found himself shaking his head. Perhaps with time and training Adan could become something more, but personalities were hard to change, and it took more than good sim scores to be a good commander.

Dominic sighed and swiveled his chair back to gaze down on Firea. He would have to keep looking, but for now it seemed he was stuck with the job of leading humanity's last remaining forces to a dubious end.

What an honor, the overlord thought, and absently he wondered how the history books would favor him and his last command of the Imperium, but then he realized that he didn't have to worry about that, because it was more than likely that there would be no history books to speak about him.

Not human ones anyway.

Chapter 11

Ethan awoke in darkness to the blaring noise of an alert siren. Together with the siren, a computerized voice droned on, "Lieutenant Adan Reese, report to the ready room. Lieutenant Adan Reese, report to the ready room. . . ." He sat up and rubbed his eyes tiredly. *What time is it?* he wondered. "Lieutenant Adan Reese, report to—"

"All right, I'm up already!"

The alarm cut off, and the lights came on automatically, blinding him with their brightness. Ethan blinked a few times quickly and looked around a small, unfamiliar room with dark gray walls. He lay on a single bunk. Opposite him, at the foot of the bed, was a locker, and hanging on the walls were a few photos of people and places he didn't recognize.

His head was pounding, and his nose felt stuffy. Ethan pressed a hand to his forehead and squinted his eyes shut. He didn't even know where he was. What had happened last night?

Then he remembered: he'd stayed up until late, drinking Mavericks in a rec hall called "The Basement" and his name wasn't Adan Reese. That was the name of the pilot he was pretending to be so he could sabotage the *Valiant*.

Ethan looked down at himself and found that he'd fallen

asleep in his uniform, which meant he still had the holoskin on. That was good; at least he wouldn't have to go through the elaborate process of putting it on before heading to the ready room.

As he thought it over, Ethan wondered why he was being summoned there at all. The commander had told him he'd have a few days leave, so this had to be an emergency. Pushing himself out of bed with a groan, Ethan stumbled over to the locker in search of pills for his headache. He opened it and rummaged around through Adan's things until he found a first aid kit. Inside there were a few painkillers. Ethan popped two in his mouth and turned in a dizzy circle to find the bathroom. Once he located it, he stumbled through the narrow door and turned on the sink so he could swallow the pill, but once his lips brushed the water he awoke an incredible thirst, and he just left the sink running while he lapped up great mouthfuls of water.

When he was done, Ethan felt slightly better, but his nose was still stuffed up and his headache hadn't disappeared yet. He didn't have time to worry about that, though. First, he needed to make his way to the ready room and see what was up.

As Ethan hurried out of his quarters, he became aware of a growing tickle in his throat, and soon he was coughing uncontrollably. Ethan frowned. He must've come down with something. He'd have to remember to find the med bay so he could request a few Viruxem to deal with the virus, and maybe while he was at it, a Soberanta for his hangover.

Ethan looked around the corridor beyond his quarters, wondering which way to the ready room—left or right, but he didn't recognize where he was at all. Fortunately for him, doors were swishing open all around him and pilots were spilling out into the corridor at a rapid rate. He followed them to the rail car system and boarded the next car with the rest of the pilots. He didn't recognize any of them, so he kept his mouth shut and found an empty corner of the rail car and slumped down there. Before long, one of the pilots came up and sat next to him.

"Hoi there!"

Ethan looked up with a scowl. "Hoi."

The other pilot, a curly-haired blond with an irritating smile and a small, skinny frame raised his eyebrows. "You look like death."

"What a coincidence—that's how I feel, too."

"You should take something for that."

"Just dropped a few oxas down the hatch. What do you suppose the scramble is about, brua?"

Curly-hair shook his head. "No idea. Hey, you're Adan Reese, right? I saw your simulator scores from the Rokan Defense. Pretty impressive."

Ethan nodded. "Thanks."

Curly-hair grinned and thrust out a hand. "Taz Fontaine."

Ethan reluctantly took the proffered hand, but the man squeezed too close to his still-bandaged wrist, where his identichip had been replaced with Adan's, and Ethan winced from the pain. "You can call me Skidmark."

Taz sat down with a frown. "All right, then, Skidmark it is. You feeling okay? You don't look too good."

"Long night."

Taz grinned once more. "Had some fun, did we?"

Ethan smirked. "Not sure. I can't remember, but the Mavericks sure had fun with me."

Taz laughed and slapped him on the back in an irritating fashion. The rail car sounded out with, "Coming up on, *Pilots'*

Center," and a few seconds later, it screeched to a halt. The rail car doors opened, and Ethan slowly stood up from his seat. He and the rest of the pilots spilled out in a rush. Taz waved goodbye, saying, "See you in the ready room!"

Ethan smiled and nodded politely. He tried in vain to keep up at the tail end of the group as they hurried down the corridor to the ready room at the far end of the hall, but the rest of the pilots all outran him, and Ethan was the last one through the doors. He ended up leaning dizzily on the door jamb for support and stifling a fit of coughing which drew a lot of unwelcome attention from nearby pilots.

The ready room was set up in an auditorium style with tiered seating for more than 100 people. Ethan descended the stairs slowly, his gaze searching the rows of seats for someone he recognized. After a moment, he picked out Ithicus Adari's head sticking out above the other pilots, and he angled that way. Finding the correct row, Ethan sat down on the end and directed his attention to the man standing on the podium below. By the three glittering gold chevrons and a nova emblazoned on his shoulder, Ethan recognized that the man on the podium was a Wing Commander, the second highest rank in starfighter command. Whatever was going on, it was serious. Looking around the ready room, Ethan estimated there were over thirty pilots gathered, which had to be all the pilots currently aboard the *Valiant.*

Someone grabbed Ethan's shoulder, and he turned to the aisle to find himself facing none other than his squadron commander, Vance "Scorcher" Rangel.

The commander took one look at him and shook his head. "What did you do last night?" Vance whispered fiercely. "I told you to get some rest. Your eyes are red, your uniform is wrinkled like you slept in it, and—" the commander scrunched up his nose and leaned closer to sniff the air around Ethan. "—you smell like beer. Get out of here! I'll have a word with you in my office when I come back."

"Yes, sir," Ethan said hoarsely just before breaking into another fit of coughing that had the commander cringing away from him. That short run to the ready room certainly hadn't done him any good.

"Listen to you! I could have you drummed out the fleet just for trying to fly in such a state! Get out of here before I report you myself!" Vance said, pointing to the door.

Ethan grimaced. "Yes, sir." *So much for keeping a low profile.*

A few pilots in the nearby rows had turned to look, their attention drawn by the commotion. Then the briefing began. The room fell into darkness, and a holoscreen at the front of the room glowed to life, showing an angry red image of the Firebelt Nebula. Under the cover of darkness, Ethan slowly stood and started back up the stairs to the ready room doors. As he left, he heard the wing commander begin speaking—

"While we were asleep last night, someone seeded our SLS buoys with a virus. Our mission is to reset them all, and keep an eye out for whoever did this. Without gates to open wormholes for us, the fuel cost will be high, so we'll be making multiple trips back to refuel. Hopefully, we can reset all the buoys before the day is out, but that will depend on how fast our codes slicers are able to reset them. Any questions?"

Ethan walked through the doors and out the ready room before he had a chance to hear the first question. It didn't sound like he was missing much. It would be a boring, tedious mission, and if anything, being forced to stay behind would give him more of an opportunity to sabotage the *Valiant*. Ethan grinned as he made his way back to the rail car system at the end of the corridor. The commander could threaten all he wanted to drum him out of the fleet, but at the end of the day, there wasn't going to be a fleet to get drummed out of.

His conscience gave him a pang with that vindictive thought, and he shook his head. What was he thinking? He wasn't even in the fleet. Besides, he reminded himself, he wasn't looking for a way to kill the crew—just a way to doom their ship. No one would get hurt.

No sooner had Ethan finished that thought than he began coughing uncontrollably again. He reached the rail car tunnel and punched the summon car button. *Maybe I'd better find the med bay first,* he decided. When the tunnel doors opened to let him into the next rail car, Ethan stepped up to the directory beside the car doors and keyed in *Med Center* as his destination. Then he found a seat in the mostly-empty car and leaned his head back against the wall, closing his eyes for just a moment. He wasn't sure how long he'd slept last night, but it couldn't have been for more than a few hours, and he was exhausted. Maybe a good stop for him to make after the med center would be his quarters for a nap. A few more hours of sleep wouldn't kill him.

Chapter 12

Ethan walked through the double doors and into the med center, past the handful of cadets, fleet engineers, and ranking officers in the waiting room, and straight up to the reception desk. The woman standing behind the desk eyed him as he approached.

"I need to see a medic," Ethan said.

"You wouldn't be here if you didn't," she replied. "Hold out your hand." Ethan gave her his right hand and turned it over to bare his wrist. The receptionist promptly scanned him with a wand, and pointed to the rows of seating in the waiting room. "Wait your turn."

Ethan found the nearest seat and settled in to wait. He felt his throat begin tickling again, and he let loose a hacking series of coughs. A few of the nearby officers glanced his way and scowled. Ethan tried to ignore them. He shifted his attention elsewhere and found his eyes settle on a shifting light sculpture in the center of the waiting room. It was casting dancing patterns of rainbow-colored light on the ceiling. Ethan focused on the fiery depths of the sculpture. He found that those shifting patterns of iridescent light soon calmed and mesmerized him. After a while, he even forgot to cough. In days gone by such sculptures had been used to manipulate a person's mental and physiological states, but he hadn't seen one properly employed since his exile to Dark Space.

There weren't many people in the waiting room ahead of him, and between his exhaustion and the strangely soothing sculpture, Ethan barely noticed them going ahead of him.

Before long Ethan heard, "Lieutenant Adan Reese," and he rose dreamily from his chair and turned to see a young male nurse waiting at the beginning of a long, white hallway. Ethan followed the nurse down the hallway to a small examination room. Inside the room, there was a tiny viewport just above the bed where the nurse directed him to lie down. The nurse promptly hooked him up to diagnostic unit and began studying the results.

Ethan's throat began tickling again now that he was lying down. He tried to fight it, but before long his body convulsed with another fit of coughing. When it was over, he shook his head and groaned.

The nurse eyed him curiously. "Well, I don't suppose I have to tell you this, but it would appear that you have a relatively bad case of the common cold. Ordinarily I would prescribe you with anti-virals and bed rest, but since you are a nova pilot and the fleet can't afford to do without you for a few days, I'm going to recommend we rather put you in a stasis tube and treat you more aggressively."

Ethan groaned again. "Whatever you think's best, Doc."

"Yes," the nurse nodded to himself, his eyes still locked on the diagnostic unit's screens. "That way you'll be back in the cockpit again in no time," he said, and flashed Ethan a quick smile. "I'll be right back with the doctor. Meanwhile, get some rest."

Ethan nodded and laid his head back against the bed. The door swished open, and then shut again, and he was left alone with his thoughts. He felt like the room was spinning around him, so he closed his eyes, but the feeling didn't go away.

His throat began tickling once more, provoking another coughing fit. *Just what I needed,* he thought. He hadn't even begun his mission! Brondi hadn't set a timeframe, but the crime boss wasn't known for being the most patient person in the galaxy. It was beginning to look like Alara would be killed before he had a chance to rescue her. Ethan grimaced. *Hurry up, Doc. . . .*

* * *

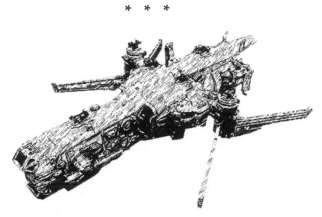

Alec Brondi watched the red clouds of the Firebelt Nebula roiling angrily in the background as they cruised back to the final SLS interrupter buoy along the Firean-Chorlis route. Brondi stood on the bridge of his corvette, arms crossed over his chest, waiting for the SLS drives to spin up again. It had cost him a lot of time and fuel to sabotage all the buoys along the Firean-Chorlis space lane. The process of infecting the buoys with a computer virus had been long and tedious, but it would be even more tedious to undo, and it would keep the *Valiant* cut off from aid for the crucial window of time that was necessary. The buoys were all simultaneously malfunctioning now, causing ships traveling from the Chorlis system to the

Firean system, where the *Valiant* was stationed, to drop out of SLS as though a dangerous obstacle had been encountered in real space along their flight path. The result would be costly delays in time and fuel for all of the ships traveling that route. It would be nearly impossible to reach the *Valiant* until the buoys were fixed, which would buy time for Brondi's other virus to take its toll.

The crime boss turned to address Dr. Kurlin Vastra, his biochemist. "You're sure that your vaccine will work?"

The old cadaverous doctor nodded slowly. "Absolutely. We won't get sick at all, not even a sniffle."

"And you're sure that the virus won't set off pathogen detectors aboard the *Valiant*?"

"No, because it is a hybrid of two separate viruses and each of them will be recognized separately as a common, non-dangerous type. Moreover, aside from our host, who is carrying a mega dose of both viruses, none of the infected will even present with symptoms. Only subsequent generations of the virus which have resulted from mixing of the two base types will produce symptoms, and although the hybrid virus *will* present as a dangerous type and set off pathogen sensors aboard the ship, by that time everyone should be infected and it will be too late. The hybrid will kill its host within hours."

Brondi nodded slowly. "Meaning that before the interrupter buoys can be reset, everyone should be dead."

"Yes, arming the buoys is just a precautionary measure to make sure none of the infected escape with the virus, which is good—just in case, mind you—because the virus is extremely virulent."

Brondi glared at the doctor. "I thought you said your vaccine will work."

"It will, of course it will. But it is always good to have a backup plan. Had we not already distributed the vaccine in the rest of Dark Space, this virus would wipe out the last remnant of humanity. All it would take is one of the infected to escape with it. After all, that is the mechanism we chose for disseminating it in the first place." The doctor held up a bony finger. "One host to kill 50,000. Rest assured, the virus will do its intended work. I must warn you, however, anyone who has recently left the *Valiant* to visit the other systems in Dark Space should have acquired the vaccine through the water supply by now, and they will survive. You will still encounter resistance among the survivors . . . though how many survivors there will be depends on the number which have been travelling beyond the Firean system recently."

Brondi snorted derisively. "Yes, a few squadrons of novas worth of resistance. The rest of the crew never leave their precious ship. The *Valiant* will have a token defense of fighters with no support crew, and I have two full wings of my own fighters to deal with them in case they want to be heroes."

Dr. Kurlin arched an eyebrow. "What about the fleet's other capital vessels?"

"They're scattered throughout Dark Space and still cut off from the comm network. Once they find out about the change in command, they'll either surrender to my newly-captured *Valiant*, or they'll be destroyed by it."

Dr. Kurlin nodded slowly. "And my wife?"

Brondi turned to look at the old man. "She'll be released to you as promised, and you can go back to engineering more bountiful crops for the agri corps if you like. Not that you'll need to with all the sols I'm going to give you."

Dr. Kurlin's pale blue eyes held a world full of pain. "You didn't have to take her hostage, you know. I would have done as you asked just for the sols."

"Unfortunately, I've found that a reward is far less motivating than a threat, and I couldn't risk you developing a conscience, now could I?"

Dr. Kurlin shook his head, and his gaze slipped away to stare out the forward viewport. "A conscience is a luxury that few can afford these days."

Brondi shook his head and grinned gapingly. "I couldn't agree more! Don't be sad, you old grub!" Brondi slapped the doctor vigorously on the back. "I'll let you visit your wife tonight, how's that? Better yet, she can visit you. Call it a probationary release, pending the success of your virus, of course."

"Yes, that would be nice," Dr. Kurlin said. "Thank you."

"Don't mention it," Brondi replied. "In fact, let's have her brought up here now." The crime boss turned to his comm officer and said, "Lieutenant Marik, have the doctor's woman brought up to the bridge to see him."

The comm officer nodded and began speaking into his headset. Brondi turned back to the doctor with a smile. "There, you see? No evil deed goes unrewarded."

The doctor gave an unconvincing laugh, while his gaze and his thoughts remained lost within the nebula.

* * *

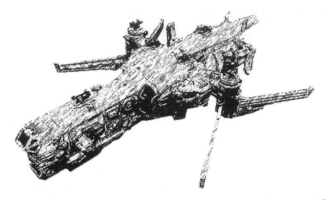

"Come on, Mrs. Vastra, you have a date with your husband tonight," the guard said, pushing her roughly down the corridor from her cell. "Hurry it up."

"To what do I owe this unusual courtesy?"

"Big Brainy must be pleased with the doc's progress."

Darla Vastra said nothing to that. She wasn't sure what Brondi had her husband working on, but she knew it couldn't be good. Her husband was a biochemist specialized in genetic engineering. His job was to help engineer more productive crops for the agri corps division of the Hydroponics Guild in order to feed the growing population of Dark Space. What Brondi could possibly want with those skills, was beyond her. Maybe he wanted to engineer a more potent stim.

Darla turned to look over her shoulder at the guard behind her. "I suppose you'll be taking me back to my cell again after this?"

The guard shrugged. "I just follow orders."

"Yes, I would expect that's what you do."

"Move along," the guard said as he shoved her forward again.

Darla was marched past a handful of empty cells on her way to the waiting lift tube at the end of the corridor. She found herself studying the empty depths of those cells as she walked by, searching for a fellow inmate, but all the cells were empty—all of them except for the last cell on the right. Inside that one was a beautiful young woman. She was sitting up on her bunk, her face hooded with long, dark hair, and her features shadowed by the cell's poor lighting. Darla felt a pang of sorrow for her. She couldn't have been more than 20 years old, and she reminded Darla keenly of her own daughter who she hadn't seen for more than a year now. Darla was just looking away when the woman sitting on that bunk stood and walked up to the cell doors. It was then that her features came into the light.

Darla gasped.

She abruptly stopped walking, causing the guard walking behind her to nearly bowl her over. He tried to shove her forward again, but she wouldn't be moved. She felt like someone had stabbed her straight through the heart. She willed it not to be true.

"Alara?" Darla asked in a tremulous voice. "Is that you?"

The guard stopped trying to shove Darla forward and instead stood back to watch the developing scene with a thoughtful frown, his gaze flicking back and forth between the two women.

The young woman's expression became puzzled. "No, my name is Angel," she said, smiling sweetly. "What's yours?"

Darla gaped at the young woman. The voice was Alara's. The face was hers, too. But she didn't appear to recognize her own mother, and she seemed to think her name was Angel. "What has Brondi done to you?" Darla asked in horror.

Chapter 13

Dr. Kurlin watched as his wife was brought onto the bridge deck. Her hands were shackled and one of Brondi's henchmen was at her back. Her posture was defiant—her chin thrust out, her back straight, and her blue eyes were glittering darkly. Kurlin knew that posture. His wife was furious. The man leading her onto the bridge passed charge of her over to the guards standing by the entrance, while he walked up to Brondi with a grave frown.

Something was wrong.

Kurlin locked eyes with his wife, and she held his gaze silently, but he had the distinct impression she was trying to tell him something. Kurlin turned to see the bodyguard who had brought her onto the bridge walk up to Brondi and whisper something in his ear, to which Brondi whirled around furiously. "Then why did you bring her here? You imbecile! Take her back."

The doctor turned to eye Brondi suspiciously. "What's the matter?"

Brondi shook his head. "Nothing."

That was when Kurlin heard his wife shout out behind him, "They have Alara!"

Kurlin turned to see his wife straining to break free from the pair of guards at the door. A moment later, he felt his own arms seized, and he turned to see a guard on either side of him.

"What is the meaning of this?" Kurlin demanded.

Brondi shook his head sadly. "I wasn't aware that she was your daughter, I swear."

"Then let her go!" Kurlin roared.

"I'm afraid it's not that simple."

"I did everything you asked!"

The crime lord inclined his head. "Yes, that you did. Thank you, by the way." Turning his attention to the guards holding Kurlin, he said, "Take them to the detention level and lock them up."

* * *

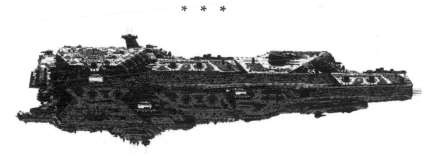

Ethan stood naked and shivering in the stasis room, his eyes drawn to the nearest stasis tube. The room was vast and airy, filled with dozens of the blue transpiranium tubes. Ethan frowned uncertainly at the tube which was being prepped for him and turned to the doctor who stood filling a syringe at a nearby desk. "You're sure this is necessary, Doc?"

The doctor looked up from his work and tapped the air out of his syringe. "If you want to get better fast, yes."

Ethan felt the tickle in his throat abruptly shift to his nose, and he let loose a violent sneeze that left his eyes watering and his nose running. "Why don't you just give me a pill," he asked in a nasal voice.

The doctor began chuckling. "Listen to you!" He walked over to Ethan and gestured for him to sit down on the stool beside the stasis tube. "Don't worry, you won't even be aware of the time passing," the doctor said as he disinfected Ethan's arm and searched for a vein to inject the stasis preparation.

"Exactly how long will I be out for?" Ethan winced as the needle went in.

"No more than twelve hours. Possibly less." The doctor finished injecting him, and withdrew the needle with a small, satisfied smile. "There! You'll start feeling sleepy soon."

Ethan was already sleepy; his eyes were slowly drifting shut as he sat there waiting. The doctor moved to key some inputs into the waiting stasis tube, and the blue transpiranium lid opened for him. Ethan peered inside. It looked like a coffin.

"Your stasis tube is ready," the doctor said. "You may climb inside whenever you feel ready."

Ethan rose slowly from the stool where he was seated. "What if you forget to wake me up?" He asked as the doctor helped him into the tube.

"There are fail-safes, but we never put the patient inside without specifying a duration for the treatment. Even were the worst to occur, and everyone aboard somehow forgot about you, the tube itself would wake you up." Ethan nodded as he settled into the tube, and the doctor appeared hovering over him with a smile. "But you don't have to worry about that. I'll be here checking up on you every hour, and if not me, then one of the nurses. Someone will be here when you wake up."

Ethan allowed his eyelids to drift shut, and he stifled a weak cough with his hand. He felt drugged. "Okay," he said dreamily. "Hurry it up, Doc. I need to . . ." An overwhelming sleepiness overcame Ethan then, and he trailed off abruptly, his lips still moving, but no sound coming out. He heard the stasis tube shut with a distant click and a soft hiss of pressurizing air. The tube grew warm and he felt his mind drifting as though he were floating away on a cloud. Soon, he was asleep and dreaming of nova fighters chasing one another in heated dogfights across the rolling green surface of Forliss, blasting one another to shrapnel and raining fire down on the agri-domes below. Ethan wanted to object, to ask why they were fighting each other, but then he found himself flying one of those fighters and his own hand was tightening on the trigger to fire a torrent of red lasers at another nova as it danced around under his crosshairs. He scored a hit and watched as the enemy's shields flared blue and then died, allowing a portion of the energy to bleed through. The port engine glow of Ethan's target suddenly winked out, sending the fighter slowly listing toward the ground. Ethan followed his target, tracking it perfectly in its downward spiral.

His comm crackled then with a familiar voice. "You shot me, Ethan!" It was Alara. Her voice was filled with pain. "Goodbye . . ." She said as her fighter plummeted to the ground.

Ethan's eyes flew wide, and he followed her down, saying. "Alara, punch out! I didn't know it was you!"

But the only reply which came back to him over the comm was a hiss of static. He watched her fighter hit the ground and explode in a huge, expanding fireball which shook his fighter with a concussive wave. Ethan screamed, "Alara!"

And then he woke up.

The stasis tube hissed with escaping air as the cover slowly rose. "Treatment complete," a computerized voice said. Ethan sat up with a shiver in the colder air of the stasis room. Gone was the tickle in the back of his throat, and he took a deep breath to find that he wasn't stuffed up anymore. The stasis tube had done its job. How long had he been in stasis? No sooner had he thought it, than the current date and time flashed up in his mind's eye, fed to him by the holo card reader implant behind his ear. Only twelve hours had passed. Ethan shook out his arms which were tingling vaguely with pins and needles, and he took a moment to look around.

The med center was dark, and despite the doctor's assurances, no one was there to greet him. Ethan frowned and swung his legs over the side of the stasis tube, wondering what had happened while he'd been asleep.

That was when he noticed the body lying face down on the floor, clothed in a bulky white hazmat suit and surrounded by shattered vials of who-knew-what. Ethan abruptly stood from the stasis tube and turned in a dizzy circle. All of the other stasis tubes were full, their blue transpiranium covers dimly lit from within to reveal the faces of their occupants. Deeper into the shadowy room, Ethan could vaguely see the white glove and sleeve of another hazmat suit, peeking out from behind a trolley of medical equipment.

Ethan shook his head, disbelieving what he was seeing. This was a dream. It couldn't be real. "Hello?" Ethan called out, and waited for a reply, but no one came bursting into the stasis room, and the body on the floor didn't even stir.

GHOST SHIP

Chapter 14

Brondi stood at the forward viewport on the bridge of his corvette, watching as the *Valiant* grew large and menacing before them. Beside him stood Doctor Kurlin, shackled hand and foot with stun cords.

"It's the moment of truth, Doctor. If those batteries open fire on us, your virus didn't kill the crew, and I kill *you*." Brondi finished that last part with a threatening look cast the doctor's way, but Kurlin gave no sign that he had heard. He stood with his shoulders hunched and eyes downcast, studying the deck at his feet.

Brondi felt a small surge of pity for the man. "I'll tell you what, Kurlin. If all of this goes according to plan, I'll re-invoke our former arrangement. You and your wife can go free, and I'll pay you the sols I promised."

Kurlin turned to look at the crime boss with wary hope etched on his bony face. "What about my daughter?"

Brondi held up a chubby hand to stop the Doctor there. "Don't get greedy, Kurlin. She wasn't a part of our arrangement. And I swear I didn't know she was your daughter. If you want her back, I can release her to you and disable her programming for a fee."

The doctor set his jaw. "How much?"

"How much do I owe you?" Brondi countered.

"One million sols."

"Okay, then let's say one point one million sols."

The doctor's eyes bulged. "I don't have that much, and you know it!"

Brondi eyed him speculatively. "Are you saying your daughter isn't worth the extra 100,000 sols?"

Kurlin gritted his teeth. "I'm saying I don't have the money."

Brondi shrugged. "That's all right. You can owe me. I'm sure I can find some or other job for you to pay off the debt."

Kurlin turned back to the viewport and sighed, his shoulders hunching once more. "Very well."

Out the viewport they could see the bright, multi-colored engine glows of Brondi's mixed type fighter squadrons, twelve and a half of them in all. Flying around them were a few supporting craft, including Ethan's precious *Atton* which was serving in this operation as a recovery vessel for pilots—should they encounter any resistance that is. And flying in front of them and slightly off to the port side was a large gallant-class troop transport carrying a substitute crew for the *Valiant*. Brondi hadn't been able to put together more than five thousand men, which was a skeleton crew at best for the city-sized carrier, but it would be sufficient for the time being.

He was placing a lot of faith in the fact that the virus he'd set loose aboard the Valiant wouldn't pose a threat to them, but all of his crew had been inoculated with Kurlin's vaccine, and just in case, they'd be going aboard in hazmat suits.

Behind Brondi, his comm officer called out, "Reaper

Squadron is in range of the *Valiant's* batteries!"

"Good," Brondi replied, and watched intently for the *Valiant's* long-range beam cannons to open fire on the squadron, but the carrier lay dark and unresponsive in the distance. Also a good sign was the fact that the *Valiant* hadn't tried to hail them as they approached, and as yet there were no novas flying out to greet them. To all appearances, the *Valiant* had become a ghost ship.

Brondi's mouth dropped open in a grin. "Alert the troops, Lieutenant Marik. We're going aboard."

* * *

At first, Ethan had a hard time understanding what had happened, but between the doctors and nurses collapsed on the floor in their hazmat suits, and the fact that he couldn't leave the med center because the ship was under quarantine, Ethan began to realize that there had been some type of epidemic aboard the ship. A quick query at the control panel beside the entrance to the med center confirmed it. "Emergency quarantine in effect. Only properly authorized medical personnel may enter and leave the med center."

Ethan frowned. How was he supposed to open the doors if all of the properly authorized medical personnel were dead? The waiting room floor was littered with motionless med workers in their pristine white hazmat suits.

It seemed like a mighty big coincidence that the mission Brondi had given him had been fulfilled without him having to do anything. Making matters even more suspicious, 12 hours ago, Ethan had been the only one who was sick. Now he was fine, and everyone else had died of a mysterious pathogen.

Ethan's frown deepened. He wasn't a big believer in coincidence. His gut told him that this was no accident. Ethan's mind flashed back to the fiery red cocktail that Brondi had prepared for him, and he felt abruptly sick.

If it were true, and he had unwittingly brought the deadly pathogen aboard the ship, then why had *he*, of all people, survived? Moreover, if he had been the carrier of the plague and Brondi had engineered that, then it seemed like a waste of effort for the crime boss to have used Lieutenant Adan Reese as a cover identity. Why not just capture one of the nova pilots, infect him, and release him? Ethan supposed that doing things that way, Brondi would have had no guarantees that the pilot would head straight back to the *Valiant*, or that he would be able to take the carrier by surprise. A nova pilot being captured and then released was sure to draw a lot of suspicion from the fleet. This way Brondi had more control over the spread of the plague, and he had been guaranteed of results.

To Ethan the more disturbing part of all this was that if it were even half true, Brondi had never had any intention of honoring their deal, and Alara's life was already forfeit.

Ethan's eyes narrowed to deadly slits. "All right, Brondi, round one goes to you, but in the second round all bets are off. I'm going to find you and kill you with my bare hands."

For the moment, however, his primary concern was getting out of the med bay and off the ship before the same thing that had happened to the crew happened to him. Ethan hurried from the waiting room, back the way he'd come. He was still naked, so he went to retrieve his clothes from the locker in the stasis room which corresponded to the number of his stasis tube. After that, he began searching the med center for survivors. The other stasis tubes were all lit up, indicating that their occupants were alive, but Ethan wasn't about to risk letting them out. If they were in there, it was for a good reason.

Still searching the med center, Ethan eventually found himself standing inside a vast medical supply room. But here, like everywhere else he had gone, there were dead med workers lying face down on the floor and no survivors anywhere to be seen. Ethan eyed the nearest body with a frown. If the med center had already been compromised, why were all of the medical personnel wearing hazmat suits? Maybe not everyone had been exposed. . . . But the number of dead med workers Ethan had encountered belied that theory.

More likely . . .

Ethan's mind flashed back to the med center doors. *"Only properly authorized medical personnel may enter and leave the med center."* Perhaps the suits allowed the med workers to move freely through the ship despite the quarantine. It made sense, but Ethan hadn't found any free suits. His eyes were drawn to the nearest body, and he shuddered with revulsion at the idea which occurred to him then.

Before he could change his mind, Ethan got down on his haunches beside the nearest body and began unsnapping the seals on the hazmat suit.

When Ethan pulled off the med worker's helmet, he saw that there were no visible signs of what had killed the man. Just in case the man were merely asleep or unconscious, Ethan pressed a hand to the med worker's forehead. His skin was ice cold to the touch, and Ethan recoiled from the body.

"Definitely dead," Ethan muttered to himself. He quickly

finished pulling the suit off the dead med worker and then climbed into it himself.

When Ethan returned to the entrance of the med center, now properly clothed in a hazmat suit, the doors automatically swished open for him, and he stepped out into a dimly-lit corridor. Ethan looked around, while listening to the sound of his canned breath reverberating inside of the helmet. There were a couple more bodies beyond the med center. One of them had on a white hazmat suit, while the other was clothed in a black fleet uniform. That meant the incident wasn't limited to the med bay.

Ethan walked cautiously up to the officer, and then he bent down to steal the man's sidearm. On a whim, he rolled the man over, but as with the med worker he'd stolen his suit from, there were no visible signs of what had killed the officer. With a frown, Ethan stood up and started down the corridor, winding his way around to the rail car system he'd arrived on just over twelve hours ago.

When the rail car arrived, Ethan stepped inside and found a few more dead officers slumped over in their seats or splayed out across the floor. He tried to ignore them, and instead focused on his destination. Using the directory beside the doors, he looked up the bridge deck and keyed that in—if anyone were still alive and in charge, that was a logical place for them to be. Access to the bridge was restricted, so the plague might not have had a chance to spread there. The rail car accepted his destination and quickly accelerated up to speed.

Ethan went to find a seat as far as possible from any of the bodies inside the rail car. Even if the bridge were similarly filled with bodies, Ethan planned to check from there using the life support systems to see if there were survivors anywhere aboard the ship, and if not, he'd abandon the ghost ship in one of the novas before someone came snooping around to ask him awkward questions. His excuse that it was all Brondi's fault was bound to sound mighty thin to a fleet interrogator, and that was to say nothing of what they'd do to him when they found out he was actually wearing a holoskin and impersonating a fleet officer.

Brondi's scheme had worked out just great for him. Without the *Valiant* in the picture, he would be rid of the vast majority of the fleet. The scattered remnant that had been stationed elsewhere would be hard-pressed to police Dark Space if some major upheaval were to take place—such as an open war between Brondi's forces and those of the fleet.

Ethan realized that was likely what the crime boss had been planning all along—some sort of coup d'état which would install him as the governing head of the sector. He didn't want to be rid of the government. He wanted to *be* the government.

The rail car arrived at the bridge after a few minutes of travelling through the network of tunnels which traversed the ship. The doors opened, and Ethan stepped out into a short, broad gray corridor lined with pipes, glow panels, and lift tubes. The double doors at the end of the corridor were jammed open with a half-crushed trolley full of hazmat suits and the remains of the suited med worker who'd been pushing that trolley.

Ethan walked up to the doors with a grimace. He stepped over the body to climb up onto the trolley and from there into the bridge. On the other side of the doors he found himself standing on a long silver gangway leading out to a vast array of forward viewports which stretched several stories high and wider than a seraphim-class corvette was long. Out those viewports he saw the Firean-Chorlis space gate and the Firebelt

Nebula beyond, while below the gangway he saw a few dozen dead officers slumped over the twenty plus control stations of the vast warship.

But what drew his attention most of all was the lone man standing small and forlorn at the end of the gangway, his back turned to Ethan while he gazed out at the stars. The man was clothed in a distinctive, pure white uniform with gold epaulets and tassels. Ethan felt a jolt of recognition. Only one man wore a uniform like that. He walked up behind the man in white and hoped his eyes weren't deceiving him.

As he drew near, Ethan felt a small spark of hope flicker inside of him. "Supreme Overlord?"

Chapter 15

"**O**verlord Dominic!" Ethan called out again, but whoever that man was, he didn't turn around. Ethan walked up beside him, and gently turned the man by his shoulders to get a look at his face.

He was gratified to see a familiar, ancient-looking countenance—the cheeks were sunken with age, and the man's hair and eyebrows were a brilliant white. His nose was pronounced, but thin and aquiline and hanging low upon his face. His eyes were fairly unwrinkled, as though he were too serious to have ever laughed, but his brow was etched with enough permanent furrows to portray a perpetually skeptical look. The old man's face perfectly matched the holos Ethan had seen of Supreme Overlord Dominic over the years, and the insignia on his white sleeve also matched the part; it was the symbol of the Imperium of Star Systems, with the six gold stars of the prime worlds arranged in a circle around a clenched golden fist in the center. What didn't match the holos was the shell-shocked look of terror in the old man's blue eyes.

Ethan gently shook the overlord by his shoulders. "What happened here?" he asked, gesturing to the reams of dead lying slumped over their control stations all over the bridge.

The overlord's lips began moving, but no sound came out.

Ethan shook him again. "Snap out of it!"

The overlord smiled faintly and said, "They're all dead." With that, he turned back to the viewport and pointed out into space. "Company's coming."

Ethan followed the overlord's gesture to a faintly glimmering silver cloud which was just visible against the dark background of empty space. From a distance, he'd mistaken those specks for stars, but here, so close to the black holes which rimmed Dark Space, the stars were never so densely clustered, nor so bright. These were in-system objects, glimmering in the light of Firean system's pale red sun. They were the glimmers of an approaching fleet.

When he looked closely, Ethan was able to pick out the more distant engine glows of the larger ships in that fleet, and he thought a few of them might be a considerable size. Ethan nodded to the approaching enemy and then turned to look at the overlord. "Bring up a magnified view of those ships."

It took a while for the overlord to respond, but when he did, he didn't even have to say the command aloud; the magnified view just appeared on screen as though the overlord had a command chip implanted—which, Ethan considered, was probably exactly the case.

The *Valiant's* targeting computer began highlighting known hull types. It was unable to recognize most of the enemy ships, since they were cobbled together from spare parts. But Ethan was able to recognize at least two, and once he did, his jaw dropped and his gaze filled with loathing. The first ship he recognized was Brondi's corvette, the *Kavarath*, and the second was his very own *Atton*. Ethan shook his head, unable to believe it. "That kakard! He stole my ship!"

"Where?" the overlord asked almost disinterestedly.

"There!" Ethan pointed to his ship. The SID code was still broadcasting his name for it, too. "That one! The *Atton!* Brondi's come to take charge of the *Valiant,* and he's brought *my* ship to the fight. I'm going to kill that dumb frek!"

The overlord's wide, shell-shocked eyes abruptly narrowed, and he began nodding his head. "The *Atton*? That's your ship?" The overlord's gaze was locked on Ethan's face, studying him rather than the approaching armada.

Ethan ignored the question and shook his head irritably. Abruptly he abandoned his tirade to search the myriad control stations behind them. "Don't we have any guns on this crate?"

"Oh, plenty," the overlord said, finally sounding more lucid.

"Well?" Ethan demanded. "Aren't you going to open fire on them before they reach us?"

"The gunners are all dead."

"There are no autos?" Ethan asked, incredulous.

"None that can be operated from here. This ship was not built for a crew of two, I'm afraid."

"You mean there were no other survivors?"

The overlord gave him a blank look, and Ethan sighed. "If you don't know, query the ship's life-support systems!"

"Right," the overlord said, and abruptly a holographic representation of the *Valiant* with the decks exposed appeared hovering in the air before them. The diagram was peppered with thousands of tiny red dots. The overlord began shaking his head, and turned to Ethan with a return of the shell-shocked look he'd been wearing a few minutes ago. "They're all dead."

Ethan squinted up at the image, watching for a green speck to appear which would signify that someone was alive aboard the ship, but that didn't happen. The red dots were so thick that it was impossible to see anything in between. Even the bridge deck where they were was a solid wall of red. "Wait a minute," Ethan said, realizing what they were missing. There should have been at least two green dots on the bridge, but the diagram wasn't precise enough to display each individual crewman with a dot. The sheer masses of red dots must have been overlaying the few sparks of green which represented the living. "Zoom in."

The overlord complied, and the image they were looking at grew larger, quickly looming over them. There were over one hundred floors on the carrier, and all of them were crowded with red dots. Not even one of them was green. But then Ethan saw it—

"There!" Ethan pointed to a lonely green speck. "Magnify that area, and bring up a tally of the living and the dead."

Two numbers flashed up beside the hologram, one in green—double digits—the other in red—five figures. Ethan tried to focus on the green number, and then on the rapidly growing number of green dots which appeared as the overlord zoomed in. "Hoi!" Ethan exclaimed. "We have 97 crew members among the living—counting us, I guess."

The supreme overlord shook his head. "How are we supposed to mount a defense with 97 men on a ship that requires a crew of over 50,000?"

Ethan turned to the old man with a patient smile. "Doesn't the *Valiant* carry two venture-class cruisers?"

Overlord Dominic began nodding slowly, and his eyes sharpened with resolve. "One of them is out on a mission, but yes."

"That leaves one for us. Those cruisers can get by on a crew of just over 200. I'm sure we could manage on a skeleton crew of 50 and launch a few nova squadrons while we're at it."

The overlord snapped into action, hurrying down the stairs from the gangway to the control stations below. "You're right."

Ethan followed the overlord. "So, disable the quarantine and tell the survivors to meet us in the ventral hangar. The *Valiant* is not going down without a fight."

"My thoughts precisely," Dominic said, already keying the ship's comm system to life.

DEFIANT

Chapter 16

"This is Supreme Overlord Dominic, to any survivors who can hear me aboard the *Valiant*. As you may or may not already know, we are in a state of emergency quarantine. The epidemic which swept through the ship only hours ago has left us devastated, taking the lives of almost everyone aboard. We are the sole survivors. But it appears this was only the prelude to a full-scale attack. We have an enemy fleet incoming, ready to take advantage of our weakness. In order to mount an effective defense, we will fly out aboard the *Defiant*. I am disabling the quarantine now. Meet me in the starboard ventral hangar bay. We launch in fifteen. Dominic out."

Ethan watched the overlord close down the comm, and abruptly the dim emergency lighting of the quarantine was replaced by a comparatively-blinding brightness as glow panels all over the bridge brightened. A second later, the red alert sirens came on, and the lighting switched back to a dim, but now red glow.

"Let's go," the overlord said, striding back from the comm station to the gangway above their heads.

Ethan kept pace beside him. "You think we have fifteen minutes before that fleet arrives?"

"If they want to land to take this ship, they still have to

blast their way into one of the hangar bays. The hangars' shields should hold them out long enough."

The doors at the back of the bridge automatically swished open for the overlord, and Ethan followed him through. Dominic stopped at the nearest lift tube. Abruptly he turned to Ethan and smiled. "I suspect you know who *I* am, but we have yet to be formally introduced. I'm Supreme Overlord Altarian Dominic."

Ethan nodded and stuck out his hand. "Second Lieutenant Adan Reese."

The overlord hesitated. "Lieutenant Adan Reese of the Rokan Defense?"

Ethan raised an eyebrow. If the overlord knew about him, his performance had been better than he'd realized. "Yes."

"Impressive scores. A pleasure to meet you, Adan." With that, the overlord accepted the handshake, but their hands missed, and the overlord grabbed him by the wrist instead. The overlord's grip fastened directly over Ethan's bandages, and he winced from the pressure.

"I'm sorry," Dominic said with a small smile. "I didn't mean to be so rough."

The lift tube arrived to take them down and they stepped inside as the doors swished open.

Ethan shook his head. "Don't worry about it. You're pretty strong for an old man."

The overlord quirked an eyebrow at him. "And you're pretty soft for a young one."

"Fair enough," Ethan said, watching the overlord punch in a floor number—deck nine. Suddenly, the floor dropped out from under them, but Ethan felt only the slightest sensation of falling as the lift tube dropped almost 100 floors through the ship's artificial gravity in a matter of seconds. The doors opened a few seconds later, and they walked out into a broad concourse which lay directly before a massive wall of transpiranium. Beyond that, they could see the starboard ventral hangar bay with the pristine gray hull of a venture-class cruiser clearly visible on the other side. The ventral hangar was truly massive to accommodate the 280-meter-long cruiser.

Ethan whistled his appreciation. "There's the elegance to this beast's brawn! Right where you'd expect to find it—hiding under her skirts."

The overlord smiled. "Indeed. Normally there would be another one right behind us."

Ethan turned to briefly gaze through a matching transpiranium wall to the empty port ventral hangar bay. After a moment, he turned back to the starboard hangar and walked up to the transpiranium wall to get a close look at the cruiser lying there. He couldn't help but run his hands along the cold transpiranium barrier separating him from the ship on the other side, as if to caress the vessel's rugged lines. "Whenever I see that ship, I see the ISS. I see 10,000 years of accumulated civilization. I see the endless beaches and crystal blue waters of Hanlay; the urban utopias of Advistine, Gorvin, and Clementa, but most of all I see the soaring, snow-covered mountains of Roka IV, the skies purpling just before a storm; I see the canyon cities and the glacier parks. . . ." Ethan turned from the transpiranium to find the overlord standing beside him, looking at him curiously. Ethan shook his head sadly. "And then I try to imagine it all gone, but I can't. I wasn't even there when the Sythians invaded. I can't imagine what one of them looks like or sounds like. Of course, I've seen the holos of the war, like everyone else, but they don't seem real."

The overlord smiled. "You speak of Roka IV as though

you've been there."

"Roka was my home."

The supreme overlord raised his eyebrows and smiled. "You're a Rokan? What a coincidence, so am I."

Ethan turned to the overlord with a frown. He hadn't realized the overlord had been a Rokan. In fact, he felt quite sure that the overlord was supposed to be from Advistine. "You mean you lived there for a few years?" Ethan asked.

"No, I was born there, Adan, just like you."

Ethan's eyes narrowed. "I didn't say I was born there. I said it was my home."

"Oh—" The overlord's smile faded. "My apologies, I just assumed. . . ."

Ethan nodded. So the overlord was actually from Roka. Advistine must have just been the official line—it would be more politically advantageous to be from a place which the majority of your public could relate to. "Were you there to watch Roka fall?" Ethan asked.

The overlord shook his head. "No, like you I also have to struggle to imagine that the galaxy as we once knew it is gone."

"Well, at least you saw some of the war." Ethan turned back to the transpiranium, his eyes glazing over as he looked out the hangar to the starless void of Dark Space beyond. "You witnessed the destruction," Ethan said distantly. "You know what it is we ran from. I keep thinking that someday my sentence in here is going to end, and I'll wake up back in my bed to find that this has all just been a bad dream."

He imagined that he'd wake up back on Roka IV, lying beside his wife Destra. He had nightmares like that. But then he'd wake up and realize that the dream had been a good one and it was reality which was the nightmare. In those dreams his son Atton would come running in and jump on the bed.

He'd tell them that they had to get up or they'd miss it. Miss what? He'd say. The avalanche! Atton would reply. Then Ethan would groan and roll over like he always did. There was an avalanche every other hour on Roka, thanks to the mining in the mountains. Soon as the miners woke up, they started blasting, and then the snow came cascading down from those rigid peaks. Ethan smiled sadly. *Then Atton will ask me to take him gliding, and I'll remind him that he has to be at least 10 before he can go gliding with me.*

Ethan sighed. "I wish I could see Roka again, the way it used to be." He wasn't just talking about the cities and the landscape, but the overlord couldn't know that.

Ethan felt a hand land heavily on his shoulder, and he turned to see the overlord staring at him intently, his blue eyes shining with suspicious moisture.

"I know," Dominic whispered. "Immortals willing, we'll see it all again someday."

"Right," Ethan nodded. "Someday." But he was never going to see his son again. Or his wife. There was no someday that could bring them back.

A few seconds later, they heard a screech of brakes and the swish of doors opening which drew their eyes to the far end of the concourse and the rail car tunnel there. They watched as the first pilots began streaming into the concourse.

"By the Immortals, I don't believe my eyes! Is that the overlord?" one of them asked.

"I think so," another said.

"I haven't seen him in years!"

"We saw him just yesterday in the holocasts."

"I meant in the *flesh.*"

The group stopped before the overlord and stood at attention. "Sir!" They saluted as one.

"At ease," Dominic said. "How many of you are there?"

One officer took a step forward and said, "Twenty-three, sir." The rank insignia on his shoulder marked him as a Lieutenant Commander. A second later, Ethan recognized him as none other than Vance "Scorcher" Rangel. Ethan's gaze quickly skipped over the group of assembled officers and he found four more familiar faces: Gina, Ithicus, Deck Commander Loba Caldin, and the curly blond-haired pilot named Taz. Ethan frowned. Most of the survivors were nova pilots.

The overlord appeared to notice that, too. "Nova pilots to my left," he said, gesturing with his left hand. "Starship crew to my right," he went on, gesturing with his right. "Engineers and technicians in the middle."

Once the assembled officers had been divided, Ethan noticed that there were only two crewmen and one engineer in the entire group.

The overlord shook his head. "Well, we have a few squadrons of novas here, but not much else."

"Let's wait for the others to arrive," Ethan said.

That was when Gina chose to speak up. "Adan, what are you doing up there?" The overlord turned to her. "Sorry, sir, but you should know that he's a nova pilot, not a command counselor."

"I'll decide what he is and what he isn't, thank you." The overlord's gaze moved on as another rail car arrived and spilled men and women into the concourse. The overlord called out once more as they approached, telling them to divide into nova pilots, engineers, and starship crew. Now there were just over fifty officers assembled, fully twenty of whom were nova pilots.

Dominic turned to Ethan. "How much time has passed?"

"Ten minutes, sir."

"They have another five, then."

By the time the third rail car arrived, all 97 survivors were assembled in the concourse, and *six* more minutes had elapsed. "That's it," the overlord said. And as if to punctuate that pronouncement, a violent explosion rocked the deck beneath their feet and rumbled ominously through the walls around them. Ethan saw the transpiranium wall of the starboard hangar jitter with residual vibrations, momentarily blurring his view of the venture-class cruiser beyond. Everyone turned to look out the empty hangar on the opposite side of the concourse just in time to see a whole squadron of Brondi's junk fighters begin pouring bright yellow ripper fire into the port hangar's shields. Lying in wait just beyond those shields were an old beat up troop transport and Brondi's gleaming black and silver corvette.

The overlord turned back to his crew. "Looks like we're out of time. Anyone with even partial experience in bridge control systems, follow me. Nova pilots, head to the hangar aboard the *Defiant* and get ready to launch. Sentinels, you can either come with us or stay back to slow them down, but I can't guarantee we'll be able to come back for you. Engineers to the flight deck with the pilots. Ruh-kah!" *Death and glory.*

And with that, the overlord turned to the starboard hangar door controls and passed his wrist over the scanner. The first set of doors opened, followed promptly by the second, and then the entire group rushed into the hangar and on for the waiting cruiser.

Chapter 17

Ethan Ortane hurriedly peeled out of his hazmat suit, leaving the constituent pieces on the hangar deck aboard the *Defiant*, and then he rushed into the cockpit of the nearest nova. It was a Mark II, an interceptor, but Ethan didn't have time to switch to one of the more familiar Mark I's. At least the speed of the interceptor would come in handy keeping him alive. As the canopy closed, Ethan punched the ignition and the fighter's reactors spun to life with a soft *whirring* that quickly rose in volume and pitch. Ethan hadn't had time to find a flight suit; he just hoped nothing happened to compromise the integrity of his cockpit.

Display screens flickered to life inside the cockpit, followed by the glowing green of the heads-up display. System reports bubbled up from his displays, and Ethan quickly skipped through them all in order to complete an abbreviated preflight check. His fighter faced out the hangar bay of the cruiser. Through the opening he watched as the half a dozen sentinels in the carrier's concourse began suiting up in zephyr light assault mechs. One of them had even managed to find a giant, 150-ton Colossus to pilot. Those six sentinels had chosen to stay behind and guard the *Valiant*. But they didn't stand a chance. The most they could hope for would be to buy time for the *Defiant*. Ethan took some comfort in knowing that at least the mechs' armored exoskeletons would protect the sentinels for a time against Brondi's thousands of troops.

Suddenly, the *Defiant's* static shields snapped to life, turning Ethan's view a fuzzy blue. Then came the not-so-distant roar of the *Defiant's* thrusters firing, and they were sliding out of the carrier's massive hangar bay and falling freely toward the ice world of Firea, far below the carrier.

In the next instant Ethan's comm system flared to life. It was Lieutenant Commander Vance Rangel. "All right, pilots. I'm sending you your squadron designations now. Most of us are strangers here, so don't complain about your squad and wing assignments. Guardian Squadron will fly out first, followed by Avenger Squadron. Guardians, you're flying in the Mark II's. The Avengers are flying in the Mark I's. Our primary objective is the troop transport. The Avengers will take it out with their torpedoes while the Guardians keep enemy fighters off their backs. Any questions?"

Ethan watched as his own wing assignment came in, and he saw that he was designated Guardian Five, and flying beside him would be Marksman Gina Giord, Guardian Six. *Great*, he thought, casting a quick glance out the side of his cockpit to see Gina already scowling at him from the interceptor adjacent to his.

Ethan gave her a mock salute and then keyed his comm to ask the squadron leader, "What's the *Defiant* going to be targeting with her beam cannons?"

"Same as the Avengers, if she can," Vance replied. "We have a shortage of officers with gunnery training aboard, but hopefully the crews'll pick it up fast enough."

"Roger that." Ethan watched with a frown as a junk fighter roared past the open hangar of the *Defiant*, spitting golden ripper fire through the static shields and rattling a few novas in their docking clamps before they even had a chance to take off. Fortunately the novas had their shields engaged.

In the next instant, Ethan heard Vance yelling over the comm. "*Defiant*, get those hangar bay shields up before they pick us off the deck!"

Another voice came on a moment later, "Sorry about that." It was the supreme overlord. "Shields are up now. The launch tubes are energized. You can take off whenever you're ready."

"Roger that, Command. Send the launch codes. We're ready."

Ethan's fighter beeped at him and the nav began flashing with a message saying, *autopilot engaged*, which was repeated by a female computer voice that sounded just beside his ears.

"You heard the overlord!" squadron leader Vance Rangel said. "Get ready! Guardians will be the first ones out the launch tubes. Remember to keep those enemy fighters busy!"

Ethan watched as the foremost pair of nova interceptors in his squadron began rising on their grav lifts. They ignited their ternary thrusters in a starburst flare of blue ion emissions, sending them jetting toward the glowing red launch tubes in the side wall of the hangar. Ethan watched out the side of his canopy as the interceptors disappeared into those launch tubes with a brilliant flash, and then the pair of fighters directly ahead of him began rising on their grav lifts. He and Gina were up next. Ethan's comm flashed with an incoming message from his wingmate, and her voice filled his cockpit. "Don't frek this up, Adan. I'm counting on you."

"Likewise," he commed back.

And then they were both automatically rising on their grav lifts and jetting toward the glowing red launch tubes. Ethan saw the opening of his launch tube rushing toward him, looking impossibly tiny for his interceptor, and he had a sudden, visceral vision of his nova missing by a narrow margin and exploding on the rim.

But the autopilot didn't miss, and he glided straight in. A second later the glowing red tube flashed brightly with a release of energy, and he was pinned against his flight chair as his nova rocketed out the back of the *Defiant* and into space. A quick glance at his HUD showed he'd already reached his interceptor's top acceleration of 185 KAPS. Ethan's targeting computer flagged half a dozen red bracket pairs for him straight away—six junk fighters flying toward him in a staggered line formation.

"Incoming enemy fighters!" Gina screamed.

They watched as the first two Guardians cruised through the enemy fighter formation, roaring at them with a stream of red dymium pulse lasers. Guardian Two attracted too much attention to herself and the enemy fighters zeroed in on her with their ripper cannons. Streams of golden projectiles converged on her.

"Get clear Two!" her wingmate, Vance Rangel, yelled over the comm. A second later, Ethan watched her fighter explode in a brilliant orange fireball, and he heard her dying scream echo through his cockpit.

Seeing that outcome, Three and Four quickly peeled off from their head-to-head with the enemy formation, leaving Guardian One alone behind enemy lines.

"Form up, Six," Ethan said to Gina. "We're going to rescue Lead. Switch to hailfires. These junkers have strong hulls, but they're not fast enough or maneuverable enough to evade tracking weapons."

"Switching now. . . ."

Ethan followed his own advice and began acquiring a missile lock on the nearest junk fighter. It was flying toward him at a pitiful 68 KAPS, and at 3.5 kilometers away, it was just out of laser and ripper range. Abruptly Ethan's targeting computer gave the solid tone of a missile lock, and his targeting reticle turned red. Ethan pulled the trigger and let fly two hailfires. He watched them jet out on cold blue contrails, and then in his periphery he saw another two launched by Gina. The missiles quickly dwindled into darkness as their primary thrusters burned out. Just moments later, bright sparks flew as those four missiles burst into sixteen smaller warheads and their thrusters engaged, each of them locking onto and tracking a separate enemy target. Almost immediately following that came a blinding pair of explosions as two of the enemy fighters flew apart. Their shrapnel caught a third, sending it careening off toward the planet below.

"Ruh-kah, kakard!" Ethan whooped.

"Nice work, Guardians," Vance replied. "Two and Three, you're with me now, form up."

Ethan watched on his scopes as the two fighters which had peeled off earlier arced back into the fray just above his and Gina's position. The three remaining enemy fighters turned and ran, and a moment later they began firing a steady stream of ripper fire at Guardian One.

Vance came back on the comm, sounding tense. "A little help here?"

"On our way," Ethan commed back. "Fire your afterburners, Six."

Gina clicked her comm to acknowledge, and then Ethan fired his afterburners to catch up to the enemy fighters. He heard his thrusters roar suddenly louder, and he felt his nova begin to shudder and shake. The acceleration pinned him against his seat, since the inertial management system was set to 90%. The exhilaration of it was a palpable force rising up in

Ethan's chest. He'd been born for this. He felt at once powerful, free, and incredibly vulnerable—surrounded by deep space, not even clothed in the protective layers of a flight suit. All that separated him from the abyss was a thin bubble of transpiranium and his skill in the cockpit. One sustained burst of ripper fire to his canopy and his fighter would crack open, spilling him into space. In minutes his blood would boil and his body would freeze as stiff as a duranium sheet.

Ethan gave an involuntary shiver and grinned. *What a thrill!*

The comm crackled. "I can't . . . keep this . . . up . . ." Vance said.

That brought Ethan back to the moment. He found Guardian One on his scopes. Vance was juking and jinking desperately in order to evade the converging torrents of ripper fire from three enemy fighters at once.

Ethan's range to the nearest of the three ticked down to five kilometers. "Hold on, Lead. We're almost there," Ethan commed back.

A few seconds later, the range dropped from five klicks to four, and Ethan began hearing a missile lock tone beep-beep-beeping from his targeting computer. He released the afterburner switch in order to steady his aim, and as soon as the computer gave him solid tone, Ethan let fly two more hailfires. He watched the bright orange glow of their thrusters dwindle into the distance, holding his breath and chewing his lip as he saw Guardian One taking fire. *They'll make it*, Ethan thought as the hailfires reached 500 meters to target. *They have to make it.*

And then Guardian One exploded in an angry red fireball.

Chapter 18

"**I**'m trying to call for reinforcements, sir, but the comm relays are down."

"Again?"

"Yes, sir."

Supreme Overlord Dominic glared out the *Defiant's* forward viewports at the roiling fireballs of fighters which were exploding all around them—both enemy junkers and imperial novas. He paced up to the captain's table and studied the holographic displays there. He saw a 3D projection of the *Defiant* in the center, with clouds of angry red junkers swarming around her while a small compliment of green novas flitted through those, spitting red pulse lasers and streaking hailfire missiles. Even as the overlord watched, one of those green novas exploded as three enemy fighters converged on it from behind. That was Guardian One. Dominic grimaced and shook his head. Here he could see the battle from a bird's eye view, and already, at just five minutes in, it wasn't looking good. There were six junkers to every nova, and half of the novas had instructions to ignore enemy fighters and line up for torpedo runs on the enemy troop transports, which meant the

12 interceptors of Guardian Squadron were facing down 12 whole squadrons of junkers all by themselves. Twelve to one. No nova pilot was good enough to survive those odds for long.

The overlord saw the enemy troop ships—a corvette and an old gallant-class hovering in the near-distance off the *Defiant's* bow. They were perfectly within beam range, but the gunners were still below decks getting their training from the solitary officer who actually had any, and it would be a few more minutes before they could open fire.

Dominic watched a whole squadron of junkers lining up on the *Defiant* and he had a bad feeling crawl into the pit of his stomach. "Comms, get the Guardians on missile defense, now! We have an enemy squadron, bearing 9-7-11 coming about on a torpedo run."

"Yes, sir!"

The overlord watched for a few tense minutes as the enemy fighters grew closer and closer to their port side. The Guardians came about and closed to within missile range of the enemy fighters, but before they could do anything, the enemy squadron dropped a volley of twelve torpedoes on the Defiant's tail. The Guardians were too far away to shoot those warheads down.

"Deploy EM flares!" Dominic yelled. A sparkling cloud of flares shot out behind the ship, but it only caught five of the twelve torpedoes. The other seven were still racing toward the Defiant's thruster banks. "Brace for impact!"

Suddenly the *Defiant* rocked with an explosion and Dominic saw the aft shields turn red. A damage report came up, warning that the port thruster was damaged and now operating at 56% efficiency. The enemy squadron roared out over the bridge, causing everyone on deck to reflexively duck. "Engineering, equalize those shields before they line up for another pass!" Dominic said as he watched the bright orange wave of the enemy fighters' thruster trails diminishing into the distance.

"Yes, sir," Dominic's chief engineer, a Petty Officer named Delayn replied. Without the cruiser's pulse lasers firing to shoot down enemy missiles, the *Defiant* was practically a sitting duck. Shields were meant to be a last line of defense, to catch enemy lasers and rippers and the few strays missiles that got through—not whole volleys at a time.

"Deck Officer Gorvan," Dominic began, speaking to his gunnery chief. "Tell our gunners that if they don't start firing now, we're not going to survive this."

"Yes, sir. I'll try to hurry them, sir."

Dominic looked up from the captain's table to see his XO staring grimly back at him from the other side. She was Deck Commander Loba Caldin, a complete stranger, young, but still the most experienced officer left among the survivors. She was just three pay grades below a captain in bridge crew rankings, which meant she was probably the only one on bridge with any command experience—including himself. As Dominic looked around the bridge, he couldn't say that he recognized more than one man of his crew—maybe Petty Officer Ashril Grames at the comms, and only just barely at that. He thought that maybe they'd had a drink together once in the Star Dome, an officer's lounge near the bridge. On a ship like the *Valiant*, with more than 50,000 crew, mostly automated systems, and vast amounts of space, one could never hope to get to know more than a few hundred officers personally.

Suddenly, the XO spoke up, "We're grossly outmatched, sir," she said, as if he needed to be reminded. "We could retreat and come back later with reinforcements from the other systems."

Dominic shook his head. "By then they'll have control of the *Valiant*. It would take dozens of venture-class cruisers to bring her down. Even if we succeed, we'll just have a gutted derelict."

"Incoming!" gravidar called out.

Dominic's gaze dropped to the captain's table just in time to see four fighters drop out of a dogfight with the Guardians and drop a volley of torpedoes on the *Defiant* at point-blank range. The ship rocked with another explosion, and the port shields turned yellow. Dominic saw one of the enemy fighters disintegrate as it was caught in the explosion from its own torpedo.

Amateurs, he thought. *We're being torn apart by amateurs!* Dominic whirled around to face the comm officer. "Tell the Guardians they're going to have to do better than that!"

Petty Officer Ashril Grames looked up helplessly from his comm control station. "They're down five pilots already, sir, and we're being swarmed by dozens of junkers. If we keep this up, there won't be any of them left."

"What about the Avengers? Haven't they completed their run yet?"

"They took heavy fire from enemy fighter screens and pulse lasers and lost four pilots before even firing their torpedoes. More than half of that volley was shot down by junkers and AMS—only two got through. We inflicted minor damage to the troop transport's port side, but the sections sealed off almost immediately, and I'm not sure they took many casualties."

"Well get the Avengers to make another pass!"

"They're coming under heavy fire, sir, I doubt they'll survive to make another pass."

Dominic grimaced. He didn't have the command

experience for this, even though everyone on deck likely took it for granted that he did. Dominic briefly considered yielding the floor to Deck Commander Caldin, but he decided against it, since that would doubtless compromise his authority in the future.

"It's too late, sir!" another officer chimed in from the other side of the bridge, and Dominic turned to see Corpsman Goldrim, the gravidar operator, shaking his head. "Look." The corpsman pointed out the forward viewports as both the gallant-class transport and Brondi's corvette began sliding into the *Valiant's* port ventral hangar, eliciting a violent wave of blue from the hangar's shields. The beam and pulse shields on the hangar were now weak enough that they couldn't stop the enemy ships from muscling in. Making matters worse, the hangar shields would quickly strengthen once the enemy was inside, effectively preventing Imperial forces from flying in after them or making attack runs on them from the outside. They were about to be locked out of their own ship while enemy troops overran her.

"Weapons! Get our gunners to concentrate fire on the hangar shields and bring them down. They'll be sitting ducks while they're in the hangar. If we miss that opportunity, the *Valiant* will be forfeit!"

"Gunnery crews are still prepping, sir," Gorvan replied.

Dominic gritted his teeth. "I don't care if they miss and hit the side of the carrier, just get me *something*!"

"Yes, sir!"

Dominic watched as two more Avengers and another Guardian winked out of existence with roiling fireballs that looked as small and insignificant as glow bugs beside the *Defiant*.

The battle was not going well.

* * *

Five minutes earlier . . .

"Frek!" Gina said. "We've lost Lead! Frek!"

"Can it, Six. I'm Lead now. Form up," Three said. It was the voice of Ithicus Adari. "We need to protect the Avengers from enemy fighters, so use your speed to outmaneuver those junkers, and catch up to the Avengers before they have to make their attack run alone."

In the next instant the comm crackled with a message from the *Defiant*: "Guardians, we need anti missile support, bearing 9-7-11, please acknowledge."

"Roger that, Control," Three replied. "Guardians on me!"

Ethan disengaged his thrusters and flipped his fighter to point it in Three's direction before reengaging thrust. He spared a quick glance at his gravidar and found that the enemy fighters at 9-7-11 were more than 10 klicks distant. "We're never going to get to the *Defiant* in time, Lead."

"Orders are orders, Five."

"With respect, these orders are stupid. We need to defend the Avengers or this will all be for nothing."

"Stay the course! We defend the *Defiant* first. That's final, Skidmark."

Ethan gritted his teeth and shook his head. By the time they caught up to the *Defiant*, they'd be too far from Avenger Squadron to provide cover.

When the range to target had dropped from ten klicks to four, and Ethan was beginning to acquire a missile lock on the nearest fighter in the enemy squadron, he saw them erupt with a staggered wave of torpedoes. "We're too late, Lead!" Once their torpedoes were away, the enemy fighters angled off, skillfully jinking to avoid missile locks. Try as he might, Ethan couldn't get a solid tone. He watched the *Defiant* deploy a glittering cloud of EM flares, and half the torpedoes blossomed into blinding fireballs as they collided with the flares. The other half went around and through the cloud, angling for the *Defiant's* thrusters.

"Krak!" Ethan said, and then the torpedoes exploded. When the explosions cleared, they saw the *Defiant* cruising on, still alive, but one of her thrusters was trailing smoke and flaming debris.

"Frek!" Guardian Seven chimed in. Ethan thought he recognized the voice as belonging to the curly blond-haired pilot he'd once briefly met in a rail car—Taz. "This is a suicide mission! We're all going to die."

"Hoi, if those had been navy-grade munitions, the *Defiant* would be venting atmosphere!" Ithicus shot back. "She's still OK. We don't stop flying until they clip our wings. We've still got a good chance of pulling this off. Ruh-kah! On me, Guardians! Let's show these kakards they can't draw our blood for free!"

"Ruh-kah!" The rest of the squadron chorused over the comm. Ethan stayed silent. He privately agreed with Seven, but he didn't want to hurt morale any further, so he stayed in formation and fired his afterburners to keep up.

The Guardians rushed up behind the squadron which had attacked the *Defiant* and began raining torrents of red dymium pulse lasers on the enemy fighters' tails. Ethan lined up his target and pulled the trigger. One laser bolt hit with a blue splash of shields, and then the enemy fighter jinked out of the way, letting the next six bolts miss. Ethan worked hard to bring the aggressively jinking target back under his targeting reticle for a solid lock. Briefly attaining a lock, Ethan pulled the trigger again, and this time he held it down, trying to track and anticipate the enemy's movements. He felt his ship vibrating subtly with the rapid release of energy as his pulse lasers cycled at maximum speed. The sound in space simulator (SISS) in the cockpit screamed with the continuous laser fire. One in every ten bolts hit home, eliciting a blue flare from the enemy's shields. Ethan tracked his target expertly, drawing on simulator training from his youth. Moments later the blue ripples of shield impacts were replaced with chunks of debris spinning off into space. A split second later, he hit the junker's reactor and his target exploded brilliantly. Ethan grinned and started through a slow, arcing turn to find a new target. He saw a series of three more explosions blooming in the dark as other Guardians cracked open their targets. They were making the enemy pay.

A vast backdrop of stars sparkled all around Ethan's head, just on the other side of the nova interceptor's thin transpiranium cockpit canopy. The stars seemed so close he could touch them, but Ethan couldn't allow himself to be distracted by the view. He targeted the next nearest enemy fighter and brought the red brackets under his crosshairs. His ears picked up the soft click of a laser lock even before his eyes registered the crosshair turning green. He pulled the trigger and held it down, pouring another continuous stream of bright red pulse lasers into his target. Then the laser charge gauges began flashing red on his HUD, and that stream of fire diminished to a slow trickle. Ethan eased up on the trigger and switched over to missiles just as his target began jinking out of line. Enemy ripper fire sizzled off his rear shields, and Ethan broke into an evasive pattern, forgetting about his target for the moment. The sound of ripper fire hitting his shields stopped, only to start again from another angle when a second junker swooped down onto his six. Ethan craned his neck to get a visual reference on the enemy fighters. They were converging on him from completely opposite directions—a pincer maneuver that was sure to get him killed.

"Ah, a little help over here? I'm caught in a vice!"

"Roger that, Five," Seven said.

Ethan tried to hold it together as enemy fire sizzled off his shields, turning them dark green, then yellow, and finally red. Now shells *plinked* off his hull as the shields were unable to completely dissipate the energy of those projectiles.

The streams of enemy fire on his port side ceased, followed by, "That got him!" from Guardian Seven. Now, with only one fighter attacking him, Ethan strengthened his shields on the starboard side and circled around to line up on the enemy fighter's tail. A few moments later he poured freshly charged pulse lasers into the twin hulls of a blocky junk fighter whose starboard maneuvering jet was already flickering dimly. Unable to evade him, the junker took heavy fire. One of his shots punched through to the reactor, and the enemy fighter suddenly exploded, sending the twin hulls flaming off in opposite directions.

"I need help!" Gina screamed.

Guardian Three came on saying, "Four enemy fighters just broke off from the main group! They're lining up for another pass on the *Defiant!* Get them before—" The comm died in static.

"Lead?" Ethan quickly checked his scopes.

A second later Ithicus came back saying, "I'm all right. Got winged by a bit of shrapnel. No major damage. Those four fired off a volley of torps at point-blank range. Dumb frekkers."

The command channel sounded in the next instant with, "Guardians, we need a better screen than that!"

"Doing the best we can, Control," Three shot back. "We're down by five and there are at least two enemy squadrons out here. Where are your gunnery crews?"

"Cannons are coming online any minute."

We don't have a minute, Ethan thought to himself. "Six, where are you?" he asked, remembering that she'd called for help. He spent a moment checking his scopes for Gina without any luck. A cold fist seized his heart, but then he found her on the grid, cutting an evasive pattern toward the *Valiant*. A pair of enemy interceptors chased after her pouring golden streams of ripper fire on her tail. Those two were fast for junkers, and she was having trouble shaking them.

"I'm right where you left me, you dumb kakard! I don't suppose I still have a wingmate out there somewhere?"

Ethan grimaced. He wasn't used to working in teams. "Sorry, on my way now." He came about and boosted with the last of his afterburners to catch up to the enemy interceptors. Once in range, he switched to hailfire missiles and quickly dropped one on the enemies' tails. A second later he realized his mistake as he noted the proximity between the enemy interceptors and Gina's own nova. "Gina, get out of there! I just fired a hailfire on your pursuit."

"Frek you! My afterburners are tapped out! What do you want me to do?"

Ethan thought fast, even as the blue trail of the hailfire's primary thrusters winked out. The enemy fighters realized their peril and broke off from Gina to go evasive, but they were still too close.

"Reverse thrust!" Ethan said.

"They might lock on to *me* if I do that!"

Frek, Ethan thought. "Hold on!" He thumbed over to pulse lasers and targeted the distant missile, hoping he could get it before it exploded into its four smaller warheads. At this range his targeting computer refused to lock onto the missile. Desperate, Ethan raked blind laser fire over the target brackets. Nothing happened. An instant later, the hailfire exploded in four separate directions, and Ethan felt a stab of fear. Sweat trickled into his left eye and he swiped at it with the back of one hand, blinking to clear his vision. The smaller warheads flared to life and boosted after the enemy fighters.

"They're too close!"

Ethan could hear a tremor in Gina's voice. "Give me a second!" he said, switching fire to the warhead arcing closest to Gina. He hit it with a lucky shot, and the resultant explosion tore into the nearest enemy fighter, drawing flames and debris from its thruster pods. Gina's fighter rocked in the shockwave. Then the other three warheads found their marks, and the remaining two enemy fighters exploded in blinding fireballs. Ethan heard Gina scream, and then her comm cut off in static. "Gina!"

The static hissed on and Ethan felt a horrible chill creeping down his spine.

Frek! His heart pounding, Ethan checked his scopes, but they'd fuzzed out due to the proximity of the explosions. He flew through the expanding fireballs and ignored the sound of debris pelting his fighter. His forward shields quickly dropped into the red, and he feared what that meant for Gina. "Gina!" he tried again.

Then he saw her, one of her three engines still glowing, the other two flickering. Her starboard stabilizer fins had been knocked off, and he could see her cockpit canopy was striated with fractures. "Gina, for Immortals' sake, answer me!"

A moment later her voice came back to him, but she sounded weak. "I'm alive. Took a hit through my canopy. My suit's pissing air."

"Krak, how badly are you injured?"

"Not much blood, but breathing hurts like a motherfrekker. Maybe a few broken ribs."

"Fly back to the *Defiant*. I'll cover you."

"I'll never make it, not on half thrust. . . . Too many enemy fighters."

Ethan gritted his teeth. "Well, frek it! You're just gonna give up and die?"

No answer.

Ethan watched the hull of the *Valiant* growing large before them. In his periphery he spotted the *Defiant's* beam cannons opening up as the cruiser made her first pass on the *Valiant's* port hangar. Eight blue dymium beams shot out, drawing rippling waves from the hangar's shields.

A few seconds later, Ethan saw nova fighters tearing out of the carrier's launch tubes.

"Are those our novas coming from the *Valiant*?" Gina asked.

Ethan shook his head. "We don't have anyone left on board. We took everyone except for the sentinels with us."

"So those are *enemy* novas. Frek!"

Ethan had no reply for that. By now Brondi had overwhelmed the six sentinels in the concourse between the carrier's ventral hangars and he was taking control of the ship—including its considerable compliment of nova fighters and interceptors. *Gina's right. We won't make it back to the Defiant.*

No one will.

Chapter 19

Alec "Big Brainy" Brondi watched from the bridge of his corvette as his soldiers overwhelmed the ISSF mechs on the other side of the hangar with dozens of their own smaller, less powerful mechs. Brondi's own mechanized forces streamed into the hangar, firing their shoulder-mounted rockets while the corvette's and transport's turrets laid down covering fire. In just five minutes, those six pitiful ISSF defenders were eliminated—although the concourse was left a molten, debris-strewn ruin after that.

As soon as the enemy forces were reduced to steaming slag, Brondi instructed his troops to secure the shattered concourse on the other side of the hangar, and he ordered the rough dozen pilots he'd brought aboard to go see if they could steal some novas and help defend against the pitiful resistance that the Imperial Star Systems Fleet was mustering. Near as Brondi could tell, the cruiser that had been shadowing them didn't even have enough crew aboard to man its guns.

But even as Brondi thought that, he heard one of his bridge crew exclaim, "The *Defiant* is opening up on the hangar bay shields! Blue dymium beams. The shields won't last long under that assault!

Brondi scowled. "Give our fighters a new target. Tell them to disengage the novas and blast the *Defiant* to scrap. Have them launch all their remaining warheads."

"Yes, sir."

Brondi smiled and walked back from the bridge viewports to the captain's table. He swiveled the command view to see the *Defiant* running in a slow, looping attack run on the hangar. The enemy's fighter screen was now just 10 novas strong—down 14—while Brondi's forces had lost no more than two squadrons. That was a reasonable kill-to-death ratio. Brondi's fighters now outnumbered the enemy by more than 10 to one—and that was soon to increase with the addition of stolen imperial novas. Brondi smiled a big, gaping smile. "So this is what it feels like to be supreme! Thank you, Dominic, for stepping aside so graciously. I think it's time to take command of my new ship." Brondi turned to address his bridge crew. "Shall we, then?"

* * *

"We're making headway," the gunnery chief said. "The hangar bay shields should be down in just another minute."

Supreme Overlord Dominic watched out the viewports as the *Valiant's* port hangar shields glowed bright blue with sustained fire from the *Defiant's* beam cannons. It was a pity his command chip implant didn't work to control the *Valiant* at this range. If he were able to take remote control of the *Valiant's* systems, he could simply lower the shields.

Dominic frowned and turned away from the viewports to study the holographic overview of the battle at the captain's table. His XO, Deck Commander Loba Caldin, stood beside him, shaking her head. "We're down to just 10 fighters. We should recall them now, before they all die."

Dominic gritted his teeth. "Another minute. We're almost through the shields."

Caldin turned to him with a scathing look that he wasn't used to getting from anyone. No one dared to look at him like that. "Sir, most of the enemy troops are already aboard. We can't do anything to further our cause by staying here, whether we bring down the shields and destroy their transports or not."

Dominic looked up with a hollow-eyed expression. "We have to do *something!*"

She shook her head. "We need to retreat, or we're all going to die."

"Hoi!"

Dominic recognized the voice of the gravidar operator, Corpsman Goldrim, and he turned to face the man.

Goldrim was working furiously at his station. "We have enemy novas launching from the *Valiant!*" he said.

That decided it for Dominic. He took one look at the captain's table, and then sighed meaningfully. "Helm, bring us about. Set a course which will take us close to the Dark Space gate, but not directly there. We don't want the enemy to guess our intentions. When we get close, we're going to head for the gate at the last minute."

"Yes, sir," the officer at the helm, Petty Sergeant Damen Corr replied.

The deck commander turned to him, her eyes wide. "Sir, we don't have a cloaking device aboard the *Defiant*. If we encounter Sythians—"

"Then we'll die, the same as if we'd stayed here to make a run for the more distant Chorlis gate."

"We could make a blind jump deeper into Dark Space."

"With the Firebelt Nebula between us and Chorlis?" Dominic shook his head. "You know as well as I do that's suicide. There's a reason the route through the nebula is seeded with SLS interrupter buoys."

Caldin looked away, and she nodded. "Yes, sir."

Dominic watched on the captain's table as his ship came about. It lost its firing angle on the *Valiant's* hangar, and stopped shooting. "Deck Officer Gorvan, tell your gunnery crews to focus on shooting down missiles and fighters and cover our retreat."

"Yes, sir."

"Helm, bring us up to full speed and fire the afterburners."

"Yes, sir."

"Engineering, give me more power to shields and engines! Rob energy from the comms, sensors, weapons, and nonessential shipboard functions, but keep pulse lasers strong enough for missile defense."

The glow panels on the bridge abruptly darkened as the engineering officer complied, setting the ship's systems to a low power mode.

"Comms, tell our fighters to cover us to the gate and then get aboard in a hurry."

The comm officer nodded.

"You made the right choice, sir," Caldin said.

"Hmmm," Dominic rubbed his chin. "Then why does it feel like the wrong one?"

"You're abandoning your ship. That never feels right."

"ETA to the gate, 18 minutes," the helm reported.

"Good," Dominic replied. "Let's hope we make it."

As if to punctuate his words, an ominous rumble sounded through the ship as a lone enemy torpedo escaped the *Defiant's* pulse lasers and slammed into her starboard maneuvering thruster.

It's going to be close, the overlord thought.

* * *

"Gina, you don't have a choice! I'll fly in with you, but it's now or never."

"Frek, Adan, this is the worst bad idea you've ever had."

"They're not going to expect us to land with two lone fighters. That's suicide. But we'd better move fast if we're going to make it before they raise the shields on the starboard hangar."

The overlord had dropped the *Valiant's* starboard hangar shields in order to fly out in the *Defiant*, and as far as Ethan knew, they were still down. It was just a small piece of luck that at the time Brondi hadn't realized he could fly his landing party around and land inside the unshielded hangar, but now that oversight would be of great use to Ethan and Gina.

They cruised underneath the belly of the massive warship, staying as close to the hull as they dared, so that no enemy fighters would easily pick them up on scopes. So far they were clear, but Ethan had throttled back to 51% in order to keep pace with Gina's nova and its badly damaged thrusters. At that speed they were practically sitting ducks.

Ethan had a bad feeling as they crested the other side of the carrier that they were about to run into a whole enemy squadron just lying there waiting for them.

He watched his scopes with anxious anticipation, but there was no sign of the enemy.

Ethan commed Gina. "Ready? On my mark we're going to loop back and into the hangar bay. Keep a thumb ready on your braking thrusters. We're going in hot."

Ethan heard Gina sigh. "I'm ready when you are, Skidmark." Ethan waited a few more seconds for them to get some distance from the carrier, and then he called out, "Mark!"

They both pulled back on their flight sticks at the same time, pulling a half loop which put them upside down and heading straight for the hangar. Ethan realized a little too late that he hadn't had a chance to check whether or not the shields were back up. If they were, his fighter would explode on the shields rather than fly into the hangar.

Ethan gritted his teeth and triggered his braking thrusters to slow down. He and Gina reached the static shields a split second later—

And passed straight through. Ethan breathed a deep sigh of relief as the *Valiant's* grav guns seized control of their fighters and guided them down to a long strip along the side of the empty venture-class hangar.

Ethan killed his nova's thrusters and waited for the carrier's autopilot guide him down to the deck. He deployed landing struts and watched as his and Gina's interceptors were further slowed, rolled over, and gradually lowered to the deck until they settled down with well-synchronized *thud-unks*.

Ethan popped the seals on his canopy, even before the carrier's mag clamps seized his ship's landing struts. He reached for his sidearm, but so far there was no sign of Brondi's troops milling about. They obviously weren't worried about guarding their backs. That would have been a major oversight were the battle in space not already so heavily stacked in Brondi's favor. The *Defiant* would never survive to make a landing back aboard the carrier and challenge Brondi for control of the ship.

Ethan hopped down from his nova and saw Gina's fractured cockpit canopy rising just ahead of him. He hurried to the side of her interceptor as she stood up slowly in her cockpit. Once standing, Gina's gaze flicked around to find and briefly watch the entrances and exits of the hangar. When she was satisfied that there were no enemies lurking about, she turned to look down at him. Ethan noted that Gina looked deathly pale, and she held a hand to the side of her black flight suit, which was slowly trickling blood out between her gloved fingers. Fortunately, unlike him, Gina had suited up before climbing into her cockpit—otherwise she would be dead rather than merely injured.

"Oh, frek, Gina. I'm sorry." Ethan's brow pinched with remorse.

"Yea, yea, you can buy me a round later to make up for it. Help me down, would you?" she managed a weak smile and then stepped over the side of the cockpit and slowly lowered herself until she was sitting on the wing of her interceptor with her feet dangling over the side.

Ethan stepped up to the side of the interceptor and she

held out her arms to wrap them around his neck.

"Careful," she warned, as Ethan began to lift her off the interceptor's wing, but she let out a shrill scream as the movement pressed heavily on her broken ribs, and Ethan set her down in a hurry.

"Frek . . ." she breathed, swaying on her feet. Ethan could see through her helmet visor that she was sweating profusely from the pain, but rather than allowing that to distract her she was back to scanning the entrances of the hangar.

"You think anyone heard that?" she asked.

Ethan turned to look now, too, his left hand dropping to his sidearm as his gaze flicked between the broken holes leading from hangar to the concourse beyond, but when no one came boiling into the hangar, Ethan shook his head. "Doesn't seem like it." He nodded to the distant slice of the hangar opposite theirs, which was just visible across the broken, debris-strewn concourse. "But we'd better hurry."

"Right."

Ethan started off at a full sprint, but when he didn't see Gina appear beside him, he stopped and turned to find her hobbling along and clutching her ribs. She was making loud grunting noises that he could hear even through her helmet. Ethan shook his head and rushed back to her side. "Let me carry you."

She shot him a deadly look. "I'm fine. Besides you need a hand free to shoot, and so do I," she replied as she drew her sidearm.

Ethan nodded reluctantly. "Fine."

They aimed for a melted hole in the transpiranium wall which separated the hangar from the concourse, and a minute later they were stepping over rubble and the still-smoking remains of the sentinels' zephyrs. The inside of the concourse was acrid with thready veils of shifting black smoke. The giant colossus assault mech which the sentinels had managed to muster as a part of their defense lay strewn in broken piles of scorched duranium and flaming pools of reactor fuel. There were also some charred meaty bits that Ethan didn't want to know about.

Miraculously, they reached the other venture-class hangar without encountering any resistance, but that was where the miracle ended. Ethan and Gina almost walked straight into a knot of three guards standing on the other side of the molten remains of the hangar's transpiranium wall.

The guards were relaxed and chatting amongst themselves—not paying any attention to their surroundings. With their peripheral vision cut off by bulky hazmat suits, not one of the three noticed anything amiss, so Ethan and Gina quietly raised their plasma pistols, took aim on the distant guards, and fired off a quick half a dozen red-hot plasma bolts. Two of the troopers fell immediately with smoking holes in their backs, but the salvo missed the third one, and he quickly turned and dropped to one knee, swinging a ripper rifle into line.

Ethan dove for cover behind a pile of charred debris, and he just barely managed to dodge a thundering burst from the man's rifle.

Gina took that split second to aim and fire once more. Her bolt hit the man dead center between the eyes, and his hazmat's helmet exploded with a glittering red cloud of broken transpiranium and vaporized blood. The man crumpled to the deck with a clatter of armor and weapons, and then the hangar was silent once more.

But a second later, they heard one of the downed guard's helmets sound out with a muffled voice. "What's happening down there, sixty six? I heard weapons' fire! Sixty six? Come in, sixty six!"

"Let's go!" Gina abruptly spun around and began hobbling toward the waiting corvette and troop transport.

Ethan jumped up out of cover and ran after her, his eyes immediately drawn to the odd five or six gleaming ripper turrets which were already facing them from the prow of Brondi's corvette and that of the larger gallant-class transport. "I sure hope those turrets aren't manned right now. . . ."

"You and me both, Skidmark."

But the turrets stayed grim and silent, glaring at them with impotent fury as they picked their way across a hangar deck which was littered with dozens of charred bodies and broken light assault mechs. Obviously the sentinels had put up a decent fight.

"Corvette or troop transport?" Gina asked.

"What do you suppose the chances are they left troops aboard a large *troop* transport, versus, say, a medium-sized corvette?"

"Point," she conceded.

Besides that, Ethan had a score to settle. Brondi stole his ship, so now he would steal Brondi's. They ran up the already-extended ramp to the corvette, keeping their eyes open and their sidearms at the ready, but something told Ethan that if they hadn't been fired upon while they'd been running across the open deck, then there was no one aboard.

They rushed through the opulent corridors of the corvette, running straight for the bridge. As soon as they were inside, Ethan turned and slapped the door controls. The bridge doors sealed with a resounding bang, and he spent a moment trying to figure out how to lock them while Gina hobbled up to the helm. Ethan gave up trying to lock the doors and blasted the controls with his pistol.

Gina whirled from the helm to track him with her sidearm. "What the frek, Ethan?" She stood panting and fuming at him. "I almost shot you!"

Ethan shrugged. "I guess we'd be even, then."

"What did you do that for?"

"Just in case there's anyone aboard. We didn't have time to clear the ship."

"I suppose we'll figure out how to get out of here when and if we survive," Gina grumbled. "Sit down and help me pilot this thing. I need you manning the guns."

Ethan ran over to the weapons console and sat down. A moment later he realized that there were no autos on the turrets. "We don't have fire control from up here, except for torpedoes and a pair of forward-facing gold dymium beams."

"And I suppose it's too late to ask you to go aft and hop in a gun turret," she said, flicking a wry glance to the smoking door controls.

"You could say that."

"Well, we'd better hope this crate has some kick ass countermeasures, then, because the minute those enemy fighters realize we're not friendly, they're going to drop a load of torps up our thrusters."

"Ahh . . . right . . ." Ethan's face screwed up in a frown, and his gaze drifted to the broken concourse lying before them with its too-low ceiling and too-narrow opening. "Have you noticed that we have another problem?"

She was too busy spinning up the corvette's reactors to pay him much attention. "What's that?"

"The shields are only down on the *Valiant's* starboard hangar, not the port one where we are now, so how are we supposed to get out of here?"

Gina looked up from her control station, saw the narrow concourse between them and the unshielded hangar, and she scowled.

Then an entire regiment of Brondi's troops came roaring into the hangar.

"Oh, frek it!" Gina said.

Chapter 20

Gina shook her head. "We're just going to have to blast a way out! Get ready to aim your torps at the starboard side of the hangar—not the shields."

Ethan nodded, his expression grim. They'd be taking a big risk that the corvette's shields would hold with torpedoes going off in such close proximity, but that couldn't be helped. The corvette rose quickly on grav lifts, and the view out the forward viewports panned away from the milling masses of Brondi's troops, now firing uselessly up at them with ripper rifles and pistols, to the hazy blue vista of space beyond the port hangar. Gina brought their nose into line just to one side of the hangar bay opening, and Ethan keyed his controls for manual targeting. "This had better not kill us, Gina!"

"Adan, just shoot the frekking torps!"

Ethan could barely hear her over the roar of ripper shells hissing against their shields. He stabbed the fire controls a moment later, and two torpedoes jetted out on abbreviated golden contrails before slamming into the wall of the hangar and igniting with a massive double punch explosion that blinded them with the initial flash and then turned the entire hangar into a firestorm. The shockwave hit them, sending flames roaring along the transpiranium viewport and kicking the corvette sideways into the gallant-class transport beside them. Ethan felt the world tilt around him with that impact, while his feet stayed oddly rooted by the corvette's artificial gravity and inertial management system. Then, abruptly, the shockwave was sucked back the way it had come, and they were pelted with a rain of charred bodies—Brondi's men. They'd been flash-cooked by the explosion, and now their charred corpses were about to freeze in deep space.

Ethan was left staring out at a now open view of space, framed with the ragged, still-glowing edges of the ship's duranium hull. Through the hole he could see drifting chunks of debris and a nearly invisible cloud of bodies—but beyond that was nothing but wide open space. As for the original opening of the hangar, the telltale blue glow of shields was gone. They'd been knocked out by the explosion.

Ethan was tempted to breathe a sigh of relief, but then he heard someone rapping on the bridge doors behind them. They turned to look, and then heard, "Open up! Surrender now or we'll blast the doors and vent you into space!"

"Frek!" Ethan said. "There *was* someone aboard."

Gina shook her head. "It's a bluff. They'll get sucked out with us if they blow the doors open." She turned back to her control station and jacked up the throttles. Suddenly, the ship's engines began roaring loudly in their ears, causing the deck to vibrate underfoot, and they rocketed out the hangar and into space.

"And if they're not that smart?" Ethan asked.

Gina shrugged. "Then we're frekked."

* * *

"The *Defiant's* shields are at 24% and holding, but they won't hold up when those novas get here!" Petty Officer Delayn said from the engineering station.

Overlord Dominic cast the man a dark look. "Get me more power to shields, then!"

By this point the enemy junkers had all but run out of missiles and torpedoes. Now they were just gnats buzzing around and ineffectually firing at the *Defiant's* shields with their ripper cannons. More worrying, though, was the odd dozen enemy novas which were boosting out after them at a blinding 186 KAPS, and since the *Defiant* was only making 102 KAPS at full boost, those novas were sure to catch up before they reached the gate. Dominic grimaced. Nova Fighters were loaded with silverstreak torpedoes and hailfire missiles, and with the condition the *Defiant's* shields were in, it would take just one of those torpedoes, or a handful of missiles getting through and that would be the end. It would be a narrow escape, if they made it at all.

"Where's our fighter screen?" Dominic dropped his gaze to study the captain's table in order to answer his own question. There were only eight novas of the *Defiant's* original 24 left to cover their retreat. They were doing a good job of keeping the pursuing junkers at bay, but in a matter of minutes they would come into range of the enemy novas, and then they would be quickly overwhelmed.

"Right behind us, sir," gravidar answered.

"Have the gunnery crews figured out how to man the missile tubes yet?"

Deck Officer Gorvan at the weapons station looked up from his controls and shook his head. "We didn't have enough officers to man all the guns, and you prioritized the point defenses and beam cannons."

"Well, take the gunners out of the beam turrets and give them a quick course on the missile tubes."

"Yes, sir."

In the next instant, Overlord Dominic spotted something strange appear on the blue grid of captain's table. An explosion ripped through the side of the *Valiant*, and hundreds of tumbling bodies vented out into space, followed by the corvette which had flown inside earlier. It was rocketing away at breakneck speed.

"Hail that vessel!" Dominic ordered. "I want to know who's in there, and whether they're friend or foe."

* * *

Ethan heard the comm board sound at the control station directly in front of his, and Gina snapped at him to get it. He hurried over to the comm, even as the banging on the bridge doors grew louder. It sounded like now they'd found a makeshift battering ram and were using it on the doors.

Ethan punched the *receive transmission* button, and the voice of Supreme Overlord Dominic boomed over the bridge speakers. "This is the *Defiant*, please identify yourselves, *Kavarath*, or we will open fire. If friend, please reply with your most recent Imperial ID code and a full deck holo feed. You have ten seconds to comply."

Ethan's mouth opened to offer the appropriate code, but suddenly he realized he didn't know what it was. He shook his head and turned to Gina. "Give me the code!"

"You know the frekking code, Adan!"

"If I knew the code, I wouldn't be asking!" he shot back. "They put me in stasis before the outbreak, and since then my memory has been skriffy."

"57-E7-43-QR-2S-QD," Gina rattled off, and Ethan just barely managed to type it all into the comm before he lost track of what she'd said.

"Transmitting feed now, *Defiant*," Ethan said back over the comm as he enabled a full deck holo feed. A moment later, the bridge of the *Defiant* appeared as a 3D holo popping out of the corvette's slanting upper viewport. Ethan saw the overlord gazing down on him in larger-than-life size. His bushy white eyebrows were drawn together, and his lips were pursed in a grave frown. "Adan? Is that you?"

"Yes, sir," he said. "Still alive somehow."

The overlord looked immensely relieved, and for a moment Ethan was afraid that the old man might cry, but his blue eyes just grew moist and stopped there. "I don't suppose you could help us out with a small problem we have? There's a squadron of enemy novas on our tail, and they'll be within torpedo range in a few minutes."

"Let me see what we can do. No promises. Our fire control is limited from the bridge, and we have some company on board, so we can't get to the gun turrets." Ethan jerked a thumb over his shoulder to indicate the persistent banging noise which was coming from the doors behind them.

"I see, well do your best—and one more thing: if you can make it, we're retreating to the other side of the Dark Space gate. We'll be dropping detlor mines behind us when we leave to keep Brondi from following, so you need to catch up to us and fast."

"Roger that. We don't seem to be attracting any attention for the moment, so I think we can pour a little extra energy into the thrusters."

The overlord nodded. "Good. We can't afford to wait for you. If you don't make it in time, you'll have to make a blind jump."

Ethan grimaced. "Understood, sir."

"*Defiant* out."

Ethan watched the viewport become transparent once more, and he took a quick look around to find the engineering control station. Locating it just to the right of the comm where he was standing, Ethan headed over there. "I'm going to try to give us a little boost," he said to Gina.

"Just don't sacrifice the shields. I'm not confident that our ruse is going to last much longer."

Even as Gina said that, a missile lock alarm sounded across the bridge.

"Go evasive!" Ethan said.

"What do you think I'm doing?"

The alarm became suddenly shrill and then an explosion rocked the deck. The inertial management system flickered, and Ethan felt a sudden, sickening lurch in his stomach before his feet left the deck. He went flying at high speed toward the ceiling as the forces of Gina's maneuvers at the helm were suddenly fully felt. Ethan had a moment of déjà vu where he remembered dying exactly like this during the Rokan Defense simulator run, and he watched his life flash before his eyes.

But then he felt something strong grab hold of him and arrest his momentum. The emergency grav guns had fired at the last second, and when his back hit the ceiling, he felt only a mild spike of pain. The IMS flickered back on, and the grav guns slowly lowered him back to the deck. "Frek!" Ethan said, recovering gradually from his shock. "What was that?"

Gina shook her head as she settled back into the helm. This time she remembered to strap herself in. "We're in trouble."

Ethan hurried to equalize shields at the engineering station—the port shields had taken a nasty hit and they were in the red at 21%. After equalizing, shields on all sides were back in the green at 87%. Ethan set the shields to auto-equalize in future, since he wouldn't always be at the engineering station to stay on top of them, and then he changed the balance of energy so that it was in favor of shields and engines, bleeding energy from the guns and secondary systems in order to do so. That done, he hurried back to the gunnery control station and switched to the missile launchers to see what he could do about those enemy novas. Scopes showed a few dozen junk fighters off their port side, taking ineffectual potshots at them with ripper cannons as they flew past. Ethan guessed that one of those junkers must have launched the missile that had shaken them so badly. Hoping they didn't have any more warheads, Ethan ignored them and bracketed the closest of the rough dozen nova fighters flying in the distance ahead of them. That fighter immediately broke formation and began jinking.

"Frek!" Ethan said. "The novas have missile lock warning systems!"

"You *know* that, Adan. You really are skriffy! You'll have to dumb-fire with a proximity fuse if you don't want them to see it coming, and just hope they don't change their heading before it reaches them, or you'll miss."

Ethan followed Gina's advice and switched to torpedoes; then he disengaged the targeting computer and set the proximity fuse for 100 meters. At that range, the explosion should still be lethal to the novas. Ethan fired off six torpedoes in quick succession in a rough circle around the enemy novas. The torpedoes disappeared into the distance on hot orange contrails, and then Ethan ran back to the comm station and hailed the *Defiant*. "Don't change your flight path for the next few minutes, *Defiant*. I have a ring of dumb-fired torpedoes closing in on your pursuit."

"Roger that," the *Defiant* replied. "We'll hold our course."

Ethan watched his torpedoes zeroing in on the enemy fighters. They reached 700 meters, and then Ethan's attention was drawn by an incredibly bright flash of red light lancing past them. Ethan looked up to see an unimaginably wide red dymium beam go shooting by them and slam into the *Defiant's* thrusters. A second later, the cruiser's starboard thruster exploded in a raging fireball.

Ethan was back on the comm in an instant. *"Defiant? Are you there?"*

Chapter 21

Emergency klaxons sounded all across the bridge; red lights flashed; acrid smoke hissed into the room; flames crackled at one of the control stations, and an officer was slumped there—motionless, possibly dead. Dominic picked himself off the floor and turned to see that the officer who was out of commission was none other than the comm officer, Petty Officer Ashril Grames. The overlord resisted the urge to punch the captain's table. Grames had been the only semi-friendly face that Dominic had been able to find among all the strangers on his bridge.

"Helm, go evasive! Don't let them target us again with that beam. Engineering, what's the damage?"

The helm began maneuvering and suddenly Dominic was wrenched off his feet again. A second too late Petty Officer Delayn at the engineering station said, "The IMS is functioning at 90% efficiency, sir."

That explained why every little twitch at the helm threatened to send everyone flying.

"And?" Dominic insisted as his XO helped him off the deck for the second time in as many seconds. If the other officers were smart, they'd be strapping in to their control stations right about now.

"We've lost our starboard thruster and maneuvering jets. Our reactor is damaged, but holding steady at 92% integrity. Aft shields are damaged and offline. The last twenty meters of decks four through eight are open to space, and the starboard engine room bled out a quarter of our fuel before we could shut it down."

"Is that all?" Dominic asked, feeling strangely fatalistic about the damage. *Is that the best you've got?* he thought. *Come on, finish us!*

Engineering responded to the rhetorical question: "No, the starboard nova launch tube is inoperable."

"And the hangar?"

"Still fine."

"That's something, at least. Helm, how far are we from the gate?"

"If we head straight there, one minute."

"Do so at all possible speed. Sacrifice shields and weapons to get there faster. Instruct the novas to get aboard if they can, if not they'll have to meet us separately on the other side."

"It's an eight-hour trip through the gate," Petty Sergeant Damen Corr at the helm remarked. "The novas will run out of fuel and fall short by several million kilometers."

"Then we'll send probes back to locate them! But we can't stand another hit like that!"

"And the corvette? Should we wait for them to catch up?"

Dominic's eyes turned glassy and distant. "Yes ... I had forgotten about them. . . . What's their ETA?" Dominic asked absently, his gaze locked on a distant star.

His XO replied, "Looks like they're three minutes from the gate, sir."

"Too long. That corona beam will be recharged before then and we'll be hulled." He turned from the viewports to the gunnery chief. "Set the fuse on our space mines for five minutes. That should give the corvette enough time to get through. We can't afford to leave the gate intact longer than that."

"Roger that, sir," Deck Officer Gorvan said.

* * *

"Oh, for frek's sake!" Gina said. "They've got the *Valiant's* main beam online!"

Ethan tried the comm again. "*Defiant?* Please respond!"

Looking out the forward viewports with his naked eyes, Ethan could see the *Defiant* ahead of them, cutting an evasive pattern toward the Dark Space gate. That much at least suggested that they were still alive. Unfortunately, they hadn't stayed still, so the enemy novas had changed course and four out of the six torpedoes Ethan had fired were way off target. The other two, however, were still racing toward the unsuspecting novas within an acceptable blast radius.

Ethan held his breath and watched.

In the next instant one of the novas let loose a torpedo of its own, firing at the unprotected and now flaming thruster banks of the *Defiant*. The rest of the enemy novas were quick to let their own torpedoes fly, and Ethan's heart sank. There was no way the Defiant would be able to either outrun or shoot down all of those warheads. He was too late.

Then Ethan's torpedoes reached 100 meters and they exploded. One of the enemy novas was caught in the blast wave and sent spinning into his wingman. Both of them exploded, and for a miracle, the shrapnel from that explosion hit the nearest enemy torpedo. It detonated with a sudden starburst of light, and that explosion fully engulfed the enemy fighter wave, setting off a chain reaction which wiped them and their torpedoes out in one fell swoop.

"Kavaar!" Ethan whooped. He gaped at all the wreckage which they were now flying through. It pelted their shields and plinked off their hull. A full minute later the supreme commander came on the comm, and Ethan could hear wild cheering in the background.

"You did it, you old frekker!" The overlord said in an unexpected breach of his usually clean language. "We're clear to the gate! Our mine goes off in five, so be sure you make it in time. See you on the other side, Ethan. *Defiant* out!"

Ethan's heart froze. *Ethan. The overlord just called me* Ethan. *He knows who I am!* Ethan spun around to see if Gina had noticed the slip, but her eyes were intent upon her control station.

"We're still a few minutes out," she said, sounding tense. "We'll make it before that detlor mine goes off, but the *Valiant's* main beam cannon should be almost charged. If it even grazes us, we're dead."

"Fly an evasive pattern, then," Ethan suggested cautiously. Did he even want to make it to the other side? If the supreme overlord knew his real identity, did he also know about Ethan's role in the epidemic which had swept the *Valiant?* There were surely some fates worse than death, and if the surviving crew from the *Valiant* found out what he'd done, even though he'd done it unwittingly, he was sure they would contemplate all of those fates for him and more.

Abruptly, a blinding red flash suffused the entire deck, and Ethan's contemplation was cut short. He could actually feel the heat of the beam radiating through the transpiranium and threatening to give him a sunburn. The air seemed to hum and vibrate all around him, and a computerized voice sounded across the deck with, "Shields critical."

And then the beam was gone, and Ethan gasped for air, feeling like someone had just tried to suffocate him with a sun.

"We're alive!"

"Barely," Gina said through gritted teeth.

Ethan watched the Dark Space gate swelling before them, growing larger and larger—the shimmering portal looked like a dark pool which they were about to plunge into, and then—

Space disappeared in a bright flash and was replaced by the streaking star lines of superluminal space.

Ethan couldn't believe it.

Gina breathed a sigh. "Now maybe I can die in peace," she said, but she wasn't actually in any danger of dying—probably just in a lot of pain from her broken ribs.

Ethan shook his head. They'd escaped! They were alive! He wasn't sure whether to be overjoyed or apprehensive. What would the overlord do to him on the other end?

Suddenly, they heard a crackling hiss start up behind them, and Ethan turned to see a hot, molten red line appearing on the duranium bridge doors.

"Frek!" Gina said.

"I think our guests are getting restless," Ethan said.

Maybe he wouldn't have to worry about the overlord after all.

Chapter 22

Dominic strode onto the bridge of the *Defiant* with a scowl. He stopped in front of the captain's table and gave a quick nod to his XO who was already standing there, waiting for him. He'd had a very rocky night's sleep while they were travelling through SLS. In the subsequent hours after the ship had dropped out of superluminal, and while they were waiting on the other side of the gate for emergency repair crews to finish crawling over the outside of the hull, he'd awoken briefly to give his bridge crew orders, sending out search and rescue shuttles to find their missing nova pilots. Now, just a few minutes ago, his comm officer had roused him once more with the news that all of their fighters had been found—just six of them. According to the pilots, the other two had been taken out by junkers just before they could make the jump to Sythian Space.

Dominic turned from the captain's table to Deck Officer Grimsby, the replacement comm officer. "Have we seen any sign of the corvette which was following us to the gate?"

Grimsby shook his head. "No, sir, but our sensors are significantly impeded by the nebula. Perhaps they were damaged or short of fuel and they didn't make it as far as the exit gate."

Dominic turned to stare out at the gray Stormcloud Nebula which had hidden the entrance to Dark Space for the past decade. As he watched, there came a bright flicker of static discharging deep within the clouds.

"If they haven't arrived by now," the overlord began, "then we have to assume that they're gone. Helm—" Dominic turned to find Petty Sergeant Damen Corr staring at him expectantly. "Set course for the Stormcloud Transfer Station. We'll lie low there until repairs are completed."

"Yes, sir."

"Wait!" Corpsman Goldrim at the gravidar said, drawing everyone's attention. "I have contact, coming out of the Dark Space gate . . . It's a corvette analog."

Dominic whirled to face the comm officer. "Hail them!"

Grimsby nodded and began hailing the corvette, but before he could even reply, the gravidar officer reported once more, "It doesn't look good. . . . The corvette is venting atmosphere, and the bridge is open to space."

Dominic's heart sank. "So they're dead."

"Unless they suited up before the bridge was breached."

"Comms?"

"They're not responding to our hails, sir."

"Are they under power?"

"Yes, sir, but they're not maneuvering. By now they should have spotted us and begun heading this way if their intent were to rendezvous with us."

"If they are alive, then they're cut off from the auxiliary bridge controls." Dominic turned to Damen Corr at the helm. "Bring us alongside."

"Yes, sir."

The overlord turned back to the comm. "Have the hangar operators standing by with the grav guns and bring her aboard as soon as we're in range. And have a boarding party waiting for me on the hangar deck in five minutes."

"Yes, sir."

Dominic nodded and began striding from the bridge. His XO caught up to him a moment later and began speaking to him in hushed tones. "With respect, sir, you shouldn't take the risk. Let the boarders do their work. You don't need to go with them."

As they reached the lift tubes, Dominic turned to her. "I'll be the judge of what risks I should and shouldn't take."

Deck Commander Loba Caldin frowned, but then she nodded curtly. "Sir."

* * *

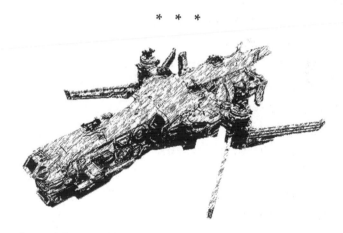

After just a few minutes of searching the ship, the boarding party found them—locked inside an escape pod on the shattered bridge.

The overlord peered grimly into the pod as his sentinels unsealed the hatch. "Hoi, there are our heroes!"

Ethan lifted his head sleepily from the single bunk inside the pod and turned to see who it was. "We made it. . . ." He noted with a groggy smile.

"Yes, you did."

Now Gina sat up beside Ethan. "Finally," she said.

The overlord jerked a thumb to the shattered bridge deck behind them. "What happened here?"

Gina spoke first: "When we realized the enemy was coming through, we set charges to blow the viewports, and then we retreated to the pod. Seems like they got sucked out into space."

"A risky plan," the overlord said.

"No riskier than a firefight on the bridge, which would have blown the viewports anyway."

"Well, come on out, then."

Ethan and Gina crawled stiffly from the small escape pod, the latter clutching her ribs and wincing. Once they were standing on the other side, they were able to survey the damage firsthand. Several control stations had been shattered by the blast, and all the viewports were blown out. Jagged pieces of transpiranium glittered on the deck and crunched underfoot as they walked around.

"So," Ethan said, giving the overlord a measuring look. "Were there any surprises waiting on the other end?"

Dominic met that look with a wry smile. "None at all, Lieutenant *Adan*."

The way the overlord emphasized his name, Ethan felt a sharp spike of dread, and he was now surer than ever that his cover was blown.

The overlord shook his head and went on, "No, everything went according to plan, and if the detlor mine we dropped did its job, no one will be following us out for a long time."

Gina snorted. "They'll have to make a new gate from scratch after that. There won't be enough constituent dust left to powder my nose."

"Sir!" Everyone turned as a pair of sentinels came striding through the melted hole in the bridge doors. "What is it, Sergeant?" Dominic asked.

"We've found three more survivors on the detention level, sir."

"Good! Release them, and bring them to my quarters aboard the *Defiant* for questioning."

Ethan was looking at the sentinels like he'd seen a ghost. There'd been people still locked up on the detention level. . . .

"Something the matter, Lieutenant?"

"No, nothing, sir," Ethan said, making an effort to hide the surge of hope he'd felt at the mention of prisoners aboard Brondi's corvette.

"Good, go get cleaned up and get some rest." Turning to Gina, the overlord took in the way she was clutching her side, and he said, "As for you—head to the med bay immediately and get yourself examined."

"Yes, sir," they said.

* * *

Maybe I imagined it, Ethan thought. *It was just the stress of battle, or maybe some comm interference. . . . Maybe he didn't call me*

Ethan. But the overlord had just summoned him for a personal debriefing—alone in his office—and that made Ethan a whole lot less sure that he'd imagined it.

That wasn't the only strange thing. They'd found three more people aboard Brondi's corvette—on the *detention* level. Alara immediately came to mind. Could one of them be her? He didn't allow himself to hope for it, but just maybe, if he were lucky—and if *she* were lucky—then she would be among those three. Or maybe she wouldn't be all that lucky. There was the small matter that now they were stranded in Sythian Space, in a damaged cruiser, and with barely any fighter escort left to defend them.

Now, five hours after being brought aboard the *Defiant*, Ethan was all cleaned up, rested, and waiting to meet the firing squad which was surely awaiting him for his crimes. He reached the double doors to the overlord's quarters and checked in with the pair of sentinels stationed there before being cleared for admittance. The doors parted with a *swish*, and Ethan stepped inside.

Unlike the rest of the cruiser, which was strictly utilitarian, this room was luxuriously appointed, and for a moment it reminded Ethan of Brondi's corvette. At the far end of the room was a broad, *wooden* desk set before a floor-to-ceiling viewport. Behind that desk was a big, high-backed black chair, which was currently turned away from Ethan to face the viewport.

Ethan stopped just inside the doors. They swished shut, and he turned to look behind him only to find that he was alone in the overlord's office. Suddenly, Ethan felt incredibly nervous and acutely aware of his skin, which was now crawling with dread. "Sir?" Ethan tried.

"Do you know why I summoned you here alone?"

Ethan felt his dread blossom into a sweaty, almost

nauseating terror, but he clamped down on it. Whatever his fate, he surely deserved it after the disaster he'd wrought aboard the *Valiant*. "No, sir," he lied.

The chair slowly swiveled to face him, and Ethan saw the old overlord steeple his hands before his lips. "I think you do. I think you know exactly why. But you don't know the half of it." Ethan watched a slow smile spreading across the overlord's lips. "What I'm about to share with you can never leave this room. Do you understand that, Lieutenant?"

Ethan blinked slowly—confused. "If you're asking whether or not I can keep a confidence, sir, I assure you that I can."

"Good, because I have kept yours. . . . *Ethan*."

Ethan's eyes bulged. "Then you *do* know. . . . How did you find out?"

"My first clue was the *Atton*."

"The *Atton*, sir?"

The overlord nodded. "Your ship."

"I see. . . ."

"I'm quite sure you don't, but let me continue. My second clue was more subtle. Few people would recognize the tells of a holoskinner—such as the way your wrist still hurts for weeks and even months after the procedure while it is accommodating a new identichip, one which you were not implanted with at birth. Few would notice that, except for another skinner."

Ethan did a double take and then shook his head. "Another . . ."

"You're not the only one who can wear a holoskin, Ethan." And with that, the overlord's hoary features shimmered and abruptly morphed into those of a much younger man—a man in his early twenties at most.

Ethan took a quick step back. "Who are you?"

The young man laughed. "That's a fine question to ask. Don't you recognize your own son?"

Ethan felt like someone had just thrown a glass of ice water in his face. "Atton?" Ethan shook his head, and his jaw dropped open. It couldn't be. This was a dream. "Is that you?"

The erstwhile overlord smiled. "Sometimes I have to look in the mirror and ask myself the very same question, but yes, it's me."

Chapter 23

Ethan struggled to understand what he was seeing and hearing. His son was alive and sitting there before him, but just a few seconds ago he'd been looking and sounding exactly like Supreme Overlord Dominic.

"How do I know you're my son? You could just be claiming to be him."

Atton was still smiling. "Then how would I know your name? You can tell me it's a big coincidence that your ship's name is the *Atton*, and that my father's name is Ethan, but I think you and I both know that's not very likely. Besides which, there's the fact that my mother's name was Destra."

Ethan's eyes widened and Atton nodded slowly. "Yes, I can see by the look on your face that I am not mistaken. My mother found the entrance to Dark Space a few months after you were exiled there. She was going to break you out, but before she could, the Sythians invaded, and she convinced her uncle, Captain Riechland, XO of the *Valiant* at the time, to take me with him when the heads of state retreated there. Riechland died in a delaying action which was to cover the *Valiant's* retreat, and I was left alone. Dark Space was no place for a young kid without adult supervision, and neither was the *Valiant*. Long story short, the Supreme Overlord took pity on me.

Later on, when the overlord was about to die, he shared his secret with me. He wasn't really the overlord. He was a holoskinner just like you and me, and so he passed the mantle of command as well as his holoskin and identichip to me."

Ethan shook his head. "You mean you're the second generation of pretenders to the throne?"

"The face of the ISS couldn't afford to die. My adoptive father's predecessor, the real Dominic, actually died very young. He passed his burden to his most trusted advisor, and his most trusted advisor—my adoptive father—passed it on to me. I was never intended to last long in the role. It was my job to find someone more suitable—someone who has all the right instincts for command, someone with the age and experience to command respect from those serving under him. That someone could never be me, but I feel fairly confident, between your actions in our retreat, and your scores in the Rokan Defense, that now I've finally found the one I was looking for. . . . Should you choose to accept the responsibility."

Ethan's eyes widened. "Kavaar . . . you . . ."

Atton held up a hand. "Please, don't give me an answer now. Think about it. We'll need some time to repair and regroup with the others out here in Sythian Space before we head back to retake the *Valiant*.

"Atton." Ethan's mouth felt dry. In fact, he felt dizzy and unsteady on his feet. He still didn't fully trust what he was seeing and hearing, but the young man seated before him was certainly young enough to be his son. "This is all a lot to take in, but you should know something before you go on." Ethan swallowed visibly and then said, "Your old man hasn't done much to improve himself since you knew him. . . ." Ethan wasn't sure how to continue. Or if he even should. He'd just been given his son back from the grave, and he was sure to lose the boy again with what he was about to say next.

Atton cocked his head. "Yes?"

Ethan smiled tightly. "I suppose I can deactivate my holoskin for a while." With that, he sent a mental command to the control system which was attached to his stolen identichip. He felt a tingle of static brush across his skin, raising the hair on his arms and legs, and then he watched.

Atton's eyes widened and he began nodding approvingly. "There's the old man I knew. My memories aren't that clear, but I can recognize you from my mom's old holos well enough."

Ethan took a few steps forward, until he was close enough to lean on the desk where his son was seated. Abruptly Atton rose to his feet and walked around the desk to stand face to face with his father. Ethan found that he was staring at a younger version of himself. The similarities between them were striking. They both had the same tall, broad-shouldered frame—the same green eyes, the same dark hair. Abruptly Ethan took another step forward and gave his son a big, bone-crushing hug. After that, they withdrew to an arm's length, and Ethan found himself grinning uncontrollably. "I missed you, kid."

"Me, too . . . Dad."

Ethan let his arms fall back to his sides. "Well, now I can die a happy man."

"Die? I hope you're not planning to die. We have a lot of work to do."

"You might not think so when you hear what I have to say next," Ethan said with a grimace.

Atton's eyes narrowed fractionally. "Go on."

"What do you think is the reason I was impersonating an ISSF officer?"

Atton raised his eyebrows and a slow smile began spreading across his lips. "The food. Our breakfast scones are to die for."

Ethan scowled. "I'm being serious, Atton. Look, I'm just going to say it. Brondi put me up to it, but that's no excuse. My copilot and I owed him a fair whack of sols. We skipped payments so he hunted us down to hold our feet to the afterburners. He kept my copilot as a ransom and said if I didn't do what he asked, he was going to kill us, so I agreed. I didn't know what I was really getting into, but ..." Ethan looked away, out the viewport, and his eyes caught a bright flash of static discharging inside the gray ice clouds of the nebula.

"What did he ask you to do?"

Ethan slowly turned back to meet his son's gaze. "He asked me to sabotage the *Valiant*. To destroy it. I was planning to find a way to doom the ship without killing everyone on board, but long before I could do that, I realized Brondi's real goal. He'd infected me with some kind of plague and set me loose aboard the ship. I don't know why I survived, but as far as I can tell, I was the first one to get sick. I went to med bay and they put me in stasis to get better. Twelve hours later I woke up and I was fine, but everyone aboard was dead. You were the first survivor I encountered."

Atton took all of that in without blinking. He was stolid and silent, as if waiting to hear the rest of the story. When he realized his father was done talking, he quietly said, "I know, Ethan. Among the prisoners aboard Brondi's corvette was the biochemist who engineered the virus. He explained everything to me already."

"Then . . ."

"I'm not going to pardon you for your sins, but since you didn't actually *do* anything, the worst we could charge you with would be impersonating a fleet officer, and possibly conspiracy against the ISS. Between the two you'd get life on Etaris, but as it happens I'm the only one who knows about your secret, and now you know mine, so we're obliged to keep each other's secrets safe."

Ethan's eyes narrowed thoughtfully. "Then there are no hard feelings?"

"I wouldn't say that. I had a lot of friends aboard the *Valiant*. Even acting in my capacity as overlord I was able to get close enough to a few people that I'll certainly miss them, but I just got you back from Etaris, and I'm not going to send you there again—no matter what you've done."

Ethan nodded slowly. "I went looking for you, you know. Both you and your mother. I went flat broke to do it, and I never found anything. Eventually I had to concede that the odds were low either of you had made it."

"The odds *were* low. They would have been infinitesimal if it weren't for the fact that Mom had already found the gate and was planning to bust you out. She was still trying to scrape together enough to rent a ship for the prison break when the invasion separated us. I've been looking for her ever since I've had the power to order missions into Sythian Space. That was the real reason we reopened the gate."

Ethan's eyes brightened. "Then you think she might still be alive?"

"She was when she said goodbye to me. Whether or not she survived is another matter."

Ethan grimaced and his gaze dropped to the floor.

"Immortals willing . . ." A long moment later Ethan looked up. "Atton."

"Yes?"

"You really want me to take command? I'm sure I'm not the most experienced commander you have, not by a long shot."

Atton shook his head. "After they all died I don't have many to choose from." Ethan grimaced and Atton went on, "But besides that, I can't imagine someone else who would be safe to share my secret with, and even if I could find someone else, that person probably wouldn't be willing to take the job, or to give me *their* identity in exchange."

"You'd like to trade, then."

"It wouldn't be a good idea to reveal myself as me; I faked my death years ago to take this role, and old Dominic's ruse is a dangerous secret to reveal. Even our most loyal crew members would mutiny if they were to discover that."

Ethan shook his head. "But I can't pretend to be the overlord forever. He already looks like he's more than 200 years old."

"You won't have to do it forever. You and I are both going to shed our holoskins before long. We'll switch to our real skins as soon as we can fake up some new identichips and a cover story for those identities. Our names will still be different, but that can't be helped. Until then, and until the overlord can formally hand over his title to you with your new identity, we're going to switch places. The *Defiant* needs a good commander if we're going to make it through Sythian Space alive, and I'm not the man for that job."

"Are you so sure I am? I probably got lucky on the Rokan Defense."

"No, that wasn't luck."

"Let me think about it."

"Take all the time you need as long as it's less than a day."

Ethan nodded and gripped his son's shoulder. "Meanwhile, I have to ask one more thing—"

"Of course."

"Was there by chance a young woman among the prisoners aboard Brondi's corvette? A young woman with dark hair and violet eyes?"

"There was. She rather takes one's breath away. A friend of yours?"

Ethan nodded quickly. "She's my copilot. I thought I'd lost her by now."

Atton frowned. "Your copilot? Are you sure?"

"Yes, why?"

"It's just . . . well, she seems more like the sort of woman to be . . ."

Ethan's eyes narrowed. "To be what?"

Atton held up a hand. "Don't take offence, okay, but she tried coming on to me—as the overlord, the old, hairy, wrinkly overlord. When that didn't work, she tried coming on to my nearest bodyguard. She's almost a dead ringer for a . . ." Atton grimaced. "Well, again, pardon my saying so, but she seems to be more suited to being a pleasure palace playgirl than a copilot."

The blood drained from Ethan's face. "Take me to her."

Atton nodded. "Put your holoskin back on."

* * *

Atton's features shimmered and back was the wrinkled countenance of the supreme overlord. "She's still being debriefed, along with her parents."

"Parents?" Ethan asked, as his own features shimmered and were replaced by those of the pilot Adan Reese.

"Yes, the biochemist and his wife. Seems like Brondi was keeping the whole family hostage to leverage the old doctor." Atton walked up to the doors and keyed them open. He nodded to his guards as he walked out, and Ethan followed him down the corridor to the lift tube at the end.

Ethan and the overlord—*his son*—stepped into the lift tube and Atton keyed in a deck number. With a gut-wrenching lurch, the floor abruptly dropped out from under them, and Ethan had to steady himself on the nearest wall of the lift tube.

"We're still repairing the inertial management system," Atton explained.

Ethan straightened with a grunt. "I can feel that."

The lift tube screeched to a halt, and again they felt the jolt, a rapid deceleration that made their knees want to buckle. When the lift tube doors swished open once more, Atton led them through the bowels of the ship, winding through darkened corridors. Every so often the corridor ahead was lit up with a hissing shower of orange sparks and then they would inevitably pass a repairman with a welding laser.

"These decks took a beating in our retreat," Atton said, pointing to a ragged patch on the near wall of the corridor where a repairman was still drawing a molten line with his welding laser to seal the patch. "We finished sealing them just a few hours before you arrived. We need to be fully battle-ready before we attempt to cross Sythian Space."

Ethan turned to Atton with his eyebrows raised. "Cross it?"

Atton waved his hand. "I'll explain later. Here we are."

They arrived at a broad set of double doors which read, *AS Pod Bay*—the aft starboard pod bay. "Where are we?" Ethan asked, though he already knew the answer.

"Our interrogation room."

Ethan frowned. "It looks like an escape pod bay to me."

Atton turned to him with a small smile "That's exactly what it is." The imposter overlord passed his wrist over the door scanner and the doors opened for him with a *swish* and a *thunk*.

Inside, at the center of the room, was a fold out table with three chairs, all three of them occupied. A pair of guards stood just beyond the doors, and lining the walls to all sides were dozens of hatches leading to escape pods. They walked into the room, and the people seated at the table looked up to see who it was. Ethan only recognized one of the three seated there, but when her violet gaze met his green, he found that not even she was recognizable. She smiled luridly at him, and gave him a well-practiced *come hither* look which he had never seen Alara use.

"Hey, handsome," she said as he drew near.

"Frek, what did they do to you, Alara?"

The young woman's brow furrowed. "My name's Angel,"

she replied, and then she smiled luridly again. "But that's all you're getting out of me until you buy me a drink."

Ethan shook his head and turned to the overlord. "She's been chipped."

Atton nodded. "It would seem so."

"Can't you fix her? Take it out?"

Atton appeared to hesitate, and then he said, "We're not sure yet. We're still looking for a cyberneticist."

The old man sitting at the other end of the table looked up then with hollow blue eyes. "Even if we find one, we'd need to know the deactivation codes, or we could turn her into a vegetable."

Ethan's gaze skipped from the old man to the old woman seated across from him, but she didn't appear to notice that they were there. Her eyes were glazed and she stared absently into the distance.

"There must be something we can do for her," Ethan insisted.

"Sure there is, handsome. Get a little closer and I'll tell you exactly what you can do for me."

Ethan winced and his gaze slowly returned to Alara's face. "I'm sorry, Kiddie."

She cocked her head and gave another lurid smile before flicking her tongue around inside her mouth in an erotic dance. Then she crooked her finger at him, indicating that he should come closer, and she blew him a kiss.

Ethan cringed.

"We'll keep working on it," Atton said. "But for now there's only one sure way to get her back to the way she used to be, and that's to beat the codes out of Alec Brondi."

Ethan began nodding. "I'd love to."

"Good," Atton nodded, and with that he turned to leave.

Ethan reluctantly followed.

As they were leaving, Alara's father called out: "What is she to you, pilot?"

Ethan turned to look back over his shoulder with a small, sad smile. "Everything."

The old man held Ethan's gaze for a long moment, his pale blue eyes glittering, his lips trembling, and then he gave a decisive nod. No further words were needed.

Ethan turned and followed his son back to the lift tubes. Once there, Atton punched the call button and the life tube nearest them promptly opened.

"I have one more secret to share with you, Ethan," Atton said as the doors closed behind them.

Ethan looked deeply troubled, and it took a while for his ears to register what Atton had said. Once they did, he turned and raised an eyebrow at his son. "Oh?"

Atton selected the bridge as their destination, and he turned to Ethan, his eyes glittering in the light of passing glow panels as the transpiranium lift tube rose swiftly through the ship on its way to the bridge. "We're not alone."

"What do you mean?"

"I mean that Dark Space is not the only human enclave that survived the war, and humans were not the first race that the Sythians conquered."

Ethan shook his head, blinking rapidly. "That's not possible."

The lift tube opened and Atton led the way back to his office. He nodded to his guards before passing through the doors and promptly locking them behind him and Ethan. With a subtle shimmer, the overlord's wizened features morphed into the young, handsome face of Ethan's son.

"Why is it not possible?" Atton finally replied. "Can there

be only one sentient race per galaxy? The Getties Cluster was teeming with life. When we sent out ships to explore that galaxy, we encountered another race that was subjugated by the Sythians. They're still alive, and numerous, but little more than Sythian slaves. They don't have a lot of technology of their own, but they are fast learners, and they are filling our ships faster than we can salvage them. We are at war again, Ethan. The war never actually ended. We need to get the *Valiant* back to help fight that war before Brondi declares himself king and warlord of Dark Space, effectively cutting us off from our supply lines."

"What . . ." Ethan's brow furrowed. "What are they like?"

"The others?" Atton asked with a smile. "They're like nothing you've ever seen or imagined, Ethan, and they are the secret to defeating the Sythians."

"I don't understand," Ethan said. "If they can defeat the Sythians, why haven't they? You said they're slaves."

"They're more powerful than they know. Would you like to meet one of them? One of the Gors? They're going to help us take back the *Valiant* in ways that you've never even imagined possible."

Ethan nodded slowly. "Any enemy of Brondi's is a friend of mine."

Atton's smile broadened, and he turned to the wall of his office. With a swiping gesture, he made a section of the wall collapse against the floor, revealing a shadowy corridor with a lift tube waiting at the end.

"Come with me," Atton said, already starting down the corridor. "And prepare to be amazed."

THE STORY CONTINUES

To Get the E-book of the Sequel for
FREE, <u>Post an Honest Review of Dark
Space on Amazon,</u> and then e-mail me
with the Contents of Your Review:
freeDS2@JasperTscott.com

*(Remember your feedback is important to me, and to
helping other readers find the books they like!)*

DARK SPACE II
The Invisible War

Now Available!

KEEP IN TOUCH

SUBSCRIBE to the DARK SPACE Mailing List and Stay
Informed about the Series!
(http://files.JasperTscott.com/darkspace.htm)

Follow me on twitter:

@JasperTscott

Look me up on Facebook:

Jasper T. Scott

Check out my website:

www.JasperTscott.com

Or send me an e-mail:

JasperTscott@gmail.com

About the author

Jasper T. Scott is the author of more than seven novels, written across various genres. He has been writing for more than seven years, but his abiding passion has always been to write science fiction and fantasy. As an avid fan of Star Wars and Lord of the Rings, Jasper Scott aspires to create his own worlds to someday capture the hearts and minds of his readers as thoroughly as these franchises have.

Jasper writes his books from a sunny paradise and offers his sincerest apologies and regrets for his long absence from the rat race, but to all the noble warriors who venture out daily into the wintry cold on their way to work or school, he sends his regards—you are braver than he.

Made in the USA
Charleston, SC
29 May 2015